JUST HOLD ON

BY

VALARIE SAVAGE KINNEY

VALARIE SAVAGE KINNEY

Text copyright © 2014 Valarie Savage Kinney

All Rights Reserved
No part of this book may be reproduced in any form without written permission from the author, except for brief quotations embodied in critical articles and reviews are permitted.

This is a work of fiction. The names, characters, places, and incidents are products of the author's imagination or have been used fictitiously. Any resemblance to actual persons, living or dead, events, or locales is entirely coincidental.

Content Editor: Leanore Elliott

Editor: Alison Jack

Book Design

By
Wicked Muse Productions

Cover Art

By
WM COVERS

JUST HOLD ON

DEDICATION

This book would not have been possible without the love and support of my family. You all mean the world to me, and I am more thankful for each of you every day.

I'd like to especially thank:
First and always my husband John, for his unwavering love and encouragement these last two decades— Having you by my side means more to me than I could possibly express, and I love you more every minute we are together. You've always been my everything.

My children: Olivia, Savannah, Donovan and Brennan—
You are my sunrise
The air I breathe
The joy of my heart
My life is so much greater
For having you in it.

My mother, Valarie—
You taught me to work hard, handle life with grace, and remain stubbornly focused on my dreams. Thank you, Mom.

My father Dale and my sister Charlotte—
Both of you always believed in me, and I would give anything to have you with us still. Each of you are lovingly remembered every minute, every day.
I loved you to the moon and back
More than all the stars in the sky
I miss you with every breath.

Mary Jo, Jennifer, Mary and Qiana—
Our Fusion Day girls
Thanks for giving all you have
So my kids can have everything they need.

K.S. Busick and G. Harris—
Thanks for igniting the writing fire within.

"CHANGES"

Everyone is facing changes
No one knows what's going on.
And everyone is changing places
Still the world keeps moving on.

Love must always change to sorrow
And everyone must play the game,
Because it's here today and gone tomorrow
Still, the world goes on the same.

It's here today and gone tomorrow
Still, the world goes on the same.

−Hugh Laurie

PROLOGUE

Smoke. The acrid stench filled his nose and mouth, burning his throat and lungs. *If I could just wake up, I could rid myself of this nightmare.* Jake fought for consciousness, but as he became more awake, more aware, he realized the smoke was becoming stronger and thicker. Something...wasn't quite right. He forced his eyes open, and saw clouds of white, filling his bedroom. This wasn't a nightmare—it was a fire.

He jumped up, fumbling through the haze for his glasses—he couldn't see without them —and feeling along the floor for the jeans he knew he'd dropped there the night before. Buttoning them, he tried to clear the panic from his brain, tried to determine what he should do next. *The phone.* He needed to find his cell phone and call for help. *No, wait, no. I need to get outside first.* Slipping his cell phone into his jeans pocket, he headed for his apartment door. He became acutely aware of a very strange sense of time passage—it seemed to him like the faster he tried to move, the more it felt like he was stuck in slow motion. Everything inside him trembled as he hurried to the door, and thoughts bounced around in his head like balls shot into action in a pin ball machine.

Jake tried to think of the things he might want to grab, in case it all burned down—his wallet, his parents wedding picture, his laptop for work. *I should grab my hat*—it started to snow last night and it might be cold standing outside, so he picked it up off the living room end table and jammed it onto his head. Just a few more steps and he would be out the door.

A pitiful sound came from the kitchen. A yelp, followed by a panicked whining and scratching on plastic. *Crap, the dog.* The three-legged rescue mutt, named Barbossa, had only been with him for a week, and he still wasn't quite accustomed to having the responsibility. Jake had forgotten the dog was even there, but couldn't just leave him to burn. He

JUST HOLD ON

stumbled to the kitchen and fumbled with the latch on the crate, then pulled a dishtowel from the counter to cover his mouth. Tucking the dog under his arm, he ran back to his door, out and down the hall.

Jake fought to see through the haze. He leaned his shoulder against the wall to help guide his path. He'd gotten as far as the third door down from his when he heard the screams.

Marnie's place, yes he remembered now, a young single mom with a little toddler girl who had recently moved into the building. His eyes and throat were burning so bad, he wasn't sure if he should finish getting out of the building, call for help, get some fresh air then come back in, or just try to help Marnie to her kid get out immediately.

Marnie's screams had become frantic, and no one else seemed to be in the hall, so he decided against waiting. "Marnie! Marnie? Open the door!"

"Help me! I need help!" Her voice sounded rough and raspy as she called out.

"Hold on, Marnie…move back, I'm going to try to break down the door!"

"Please—please, come help my baby!"

With all the strength he could muster, he slammed his shoulder against the door. Over and over and over. Finally, it gave way, and he staggered into the tiny apartment. Squinting, he tried to make out any shapes through the smoke. "Marnie? I'm here, I'm here! Where are you?"

"In here—down the hall—my baby!" Her voice sounded muffled and faint, but he was able to make it out well enough to move toward her.

The smoke was worse in her apartment than it had been in his. He opened a door to a small bedroom, and tried to make sense of the scene before him. Marnie with her thin face panicked and taut was pawing frantically at the crib...what was in the crib?

He stepped closer, and could see the baby's face with—God, was that a ceiling fan? He looked up, and sure enough, a gaping hole in the ceiling met his gaze. Shreds of wood and electrical wires dangled uselessly from the hole. He couldn't imagine how that could've happened, but it didn't matter—he needed to get Marnie and her baby out.

JUST HOLD ON

He had no idea how long it'd been since he woke up, or how long the fire had already been burning.

"Help me, help me! She's stuck."

He went to the crib, and then realized he still carried his little dog tucked under his arm. *Now what?* He could see how Marnie's chest was heaving; she kept struggling with the smoke she'd already inhaled. He could hear her wheezing as he got closer. She really needed to get out.

"Marnie, listen…look at me! I'll help, but I need you to do something. Find a window and break it out somehow. Use a chair or something. Take my dog here, get both of you outside. I want you to set him down outside and…here, take my cell phone—call 911. Okay? Do you understand me? Can you do that? Here, take him for me, I'll get your kid—what's her name?"

Marnie stopped digging at the crib slats and gazed up at him. He realized, for the first time, her hands were raw and bloody. His eyes darted to the baby bed and fan blades—they were covered in blood. His heart lurched in his throat. How long had she been there alone, trying so desperately to free her trapped child?

"I can't—can't leave Katie—I have to get her out." Her eyes looked wild and focused only on the child.

"I know. Listen, Marnie, I think I can get her out, but we need a way out of here, once I get her. Please, Marnie, take my dog, go break a window and I'll bring her to you. Take my cell phone and call 911."

Nodding, she took the little dog and looked Jake dead in the eye. "Promise me...*promise me, you won't leave here without her.*"

"I promise, Marnie, just GO!" Turning back to the task at hand, he surveyed the situation. This wasn't going to be as easy as he'd first thought. The fan blades were actually stuck inside the crib slats. He tried to think, but his thoughts were getting groggy from the lack of oxygen. He pulled, but the blades wouldn't budge, and the child appeared to have passed out. No wonder Marnie's hands were bleeding—no matter how he pulled the damn fan blades, it just seemed to get worse. He had a

JUST HOLD ON

thought, maybe he could break out the wooden crib slats. He braced his leg against the base of the crib and pulled with everything he had.

Finally! Two slats broke free. He slid his hands into the gap, lifting the fan with one hand and pulling the little girl's arm with the other. Luckily, she was small enough to fit through the area he'd broken out. He put the dishtowel he brought over her tiny mouth. Holding her against his shoulder, he ran down the hall, and was thankful to see that Marnie had done just as he told her.

A kitchen chair lay on the floor next to the smashed out living room window. He could hear her screaming into the phone, giving directions for the emergency vehicles. He hoped they would hurry.

Katie felt so light in his arms that it was easy for him to jump through the hole Marnie made in the glass. Long shards of glass stuck out haphazardly from the window frame, and a particularly sharp piece caught his jeans, but he never felt it slice through his leg. He gulped the fresh air and kept running, until he felt like he'd gotten far enough away from the building to safely lay Katie down.

VALARIE SAVAGE KINNEY

There were others around; coughing, weeping, half-clothed people. Jake pushed past them.

Marnie followed right behind him. "She's okay, right? Katie's OK?"

"I don't know! I just got out here—gimme a second..." He tried to remember the steps he'd been taught several years ago—what was it? Airway, breathing, compressions. That was it. He checked her pulse—it was faint, but there. He watched for her small chest to rise and fall, but it didn't happen. Quickly, he put his ear to her chest, listening. Nothing. *Oh, God, oh, God.* He couldn't even look at Marnie.

In the distance, the sirens wailed. Jake searched for Katie's sternum, and placing the heel of his hand there, began compressions. One, two, three, four, please God, not again, seven, eight, nine, please, please, please, twelve, thirteen, fourteen, fifteen—he stopped to tilt her head back, pinch her nose, give two breaths. He started compressions again. Why is the ambulance taking so long?

Jake lost count of how many cycles of CPR he'd done. He knew he just had to hang on until help

JUST HOLD ON

arrived—but where the hell were they? His arms were shaking and he was having trouble catching his breath, but he couldn't stop.

After what felt like hours, he sensed another person kneel down next to him in the grass.

An EMT, an older gentleman, told Jake to take a break and he would take over.

Grateful, Jake all but collapsed. He gulped fresh air as he watched the EMT check for Katie's pulse, then laid his ear next to her chest to listen for her breaths.

Why wasn't the EMT doing the breathing? "Do something!" he shouted. "Help her!" He looked frantically from Marnie, to Katie, then the EMT, who gave the slightest shake of his head.

"I'm sorry, son, but this little girl is gone, and it looks to me like she has been for quite some time. Is that her mama, standing over there?" His voice seemed kind, but firm.

"Move over, let me start CPR again. You can't just do nothing for her! You have to keep trying!"

"Son, listen. I know it's hard to comprehend, but—look at me, boy—this child is dead. There's just no more you or I…or anyone can do for her now. Now, you need medical attention yourself. You go on over to the ambulance, and I'm gonna go talk to this child's mother. I need you to tell me who she is."

He pointed to Marnie, who leaned against a nearby tree, hands on knees, trying to catch her breath. The thought struck him that she couldn't be all alone for this news, so he raced to get to her before that EMT did. As he ran toward Marnie, his eyes were riveted to hers.

She stared back at him, unblinking.

He sensed the same strange time warp sensation he felt earlier that night—the faster he tried to move, the slower it seemed he was going. Did she know what was coming? Jake reached out, connecting with her and wrapping his arms around Marnie as tightly as he could, wanting in some way to help strengthen or protect her from the truth that was only seconds away from destroying her world. There was nothing he could say; he knew nothing he could say would help or comfort her in any way at all.

JUST HOLD ON

He heard the EMT walk purposefully up beside them. He knew the man was talking to Marnie, but he couldn't hear his voice. Jake knew what the EMT must have said, the same awful things he'd heard himself just a few moments before. He felt Marnie's knees buckle. He felt sure the EMT was still talking to her, but the only sound he could hear was the gut-wrenching wailing of Marnie's voice. He thought, right then, about how he would never forget that horrible sound—it was a low, primal keening, as if it was being physically torn from her body. He didn't think it would ever stop.

Jake did the only thing he could think to do. He held on. He just held on.

CHAPTER ONE

Jake went to the funeral. He wasn't going to, but the nagging voice telling him to go, wouldn't leave him alone. He hadn't been to a funeral since—well, better not to think about it. He'd only been out of the hospital for two days, and he still felt terrible.

He hadn't seen Marnie since the morning after the fire. He stayed with her, holding her during the ambulance ride to the hospital and remained with her while she took care of the horrible things she needed to do, like concerning Katie at the morgue. Eventually, the medical staff forced Jake away, reminding him he needed stitches in his leg and oxygen. They promised to take care of Marnie.

Jake ended up being admitted for the night. He needed oxygen, and even though he hadn't realized it, he did have a large gash in his leg. Once they cleaned it up and stitched it...it hurt like crazy. He was given a shot of something to relax him, and the events of the last several hours caught up with him. He crashed into a deep dreamless sleep.

When he woke up, he asked after Marnie and was told she'd already gone home.

"Home?" he asked. "Her home burned down last night."

"Yes," the nurse...an over-nourished woman with a kind face and bifocals sitting low on her nose, replied, "But the owners of the apartment building are setting the fire victims up in another building they own. I guess the apartments were already furnished, and quite a few were already vacant. So, lucky you! I'll bring you the information before you're discharged."

Lucky me? Jake looked around the cold unfriendliness of the unfamiliar hospital room. He started to doze back off, when he suddenly remembered about the dog. Barbossa! He rang the nurse's button again.

"Yes?" She was back in an instant. "Did you need something, Jake?"

"Um—I don't know if you could help me or not—see, I had this dog, and I gave him to someone to get him out of the building. With everything that went on last night, I forgot about him and I'd just like to see if maybe there's any way to find out, if anyone found him last night. Do you know how I could find out about that?"

"Well, let me see. One of the firemen who worked in the building last night was kept here for observation. Maybe he would know something."

Thankfully, the fireman did know which shelter the displaced animals had been sent to, and Barbossa's missing leg made him easy to find. Jake felt grateful for the familiarity of the little dog as they lay together on the decidedly unfamiliar sofa in the strange furnished apartment he now called home.

The funeral had been awful. Jake thought that at least, Marnie would have some comfort from family and friends. He didn't know much about her, but he assumed her immediate family would be there to support her. Maybe even Katie's father, although

JUST HOLD ON

Jake didn't have any idea of whether or not he lived locally, or was even involved in the child's life. But surely, he would be there for Marnie?

Jake was then stunned to get to the funeral home and find only a handful of cars in the parking lot. Inside, he found the room with the tiny casket up front, and was saddened to see there were only about ten people.

The owner of their apartment building and his wife were there, and Jake recognized the manager of the restaurant where Marnie waitressed. Everyone seemed to be hanging toward the back, unsure of what to do about the scene unfolding in the front of the room.

Jake couldn't believe it—Marnie was all alone. He walked slowly to the front of the small room, toward the tiny white casket that was completely adorned with flowers. Flowers of every color he could think of, every style he could imagine, surrounded the small body inside the casket and even spilled onto the floor. There had to be hundreds of flowers.

Katie wore a beautiful dark-blue sparkly dress, with her long blonde hair, carefully twisted into two long braids. His eyes cut to the opposite end of the casket and for some reason he wanted to look away—run away. Hell, who was he kidding? He knew the reason—the sight of Katie's little black patent-leather dress shoes made his breath catch in his throat.

Jake swallowed heavily, and then he did look away, blinking for a moment to clear the burning in his eyes, the white light of pain in his thoughts. Then, he turned back to the small Victorian couch Marnie sat on. He still couldn't grasp the fact of how there was no one here to help support her.

The service was due to begin in less than ten minutes, and she still sat by herself. How could people just leave her there like this? How cold could they be? Jake stood, hands in his pockets, considering the situation for a moment.

He studied Marnie, really looked at her, for probably the first time since he'd known her. Marnie's hair looked to be a deep auburn color, and she wore it long, to her waist. Heavy and loose, it

JUST HOLD ON

seemed so tangled, it looked as though it hadn't been brushed since before the fire. She wore a ragged T-shirt and an old pair of jeans with holes in the knees along with a pair of flip-flops on her feet. It looked as though she hadn't eaten or drunk anything since that hateful night. She looked thinner with great, dark purple shadows beneath her swollen eyes. Her lips were so chapped they were cracked and bleeding, and her hands—he could hardly stand to look at them.

He remembered how raw and bloody they'd been as she tried to claw through the crib and fan blades to save her little girl. Still, they were so raw with dried, caked-on blood. Instantly, anger surged within him that the hospital would have sent her home in this condition. Didn't they know what she'd just been through?

The way Marnie sat on the couch made it seem as if she had no bones in her body; she looked limp and broken. Jake expected her to collapse at any second.

With another quick scan around the room—he still half expected someone, her mother, maybe? Or a friend, to come up to sit with her—he sighed. There didn't seem to be anyone. Jake ran his fingers through his hair, rocked back on his heels and rubbed at his stiff neck for a second, He then made his decision.

    He swallowed hard, not wanting to do this. He didn't want to care about this girl. He didn't even know her, and really didn't want to get involved to this extent. Jake already decided long ago not to get close to anyone…ever again. He knew, without a doubt, if he put himself out there, if he connected with this young woman, pain would follow.

    With another sigh, he walked quietly to the couch and sat down next to her.

    She didn't move or acknowledge him in any way.

    Jake could feel her shaking and shuddering. He slid closer and wrapped his arm around her. She didn't pull away. Jake heard the doors shut and lock for the private service and somewhere, organ music started to play.

    The few people in the back sat down quietly in seats. The pastor stood up to the podium. Jake sensed what was coming before it actually happened, which was good because he'd been able to ready himself to catch Marnie when she seemed to melt and he felt her body crash into his.

Oblivious, the pastor kept talking.

Marnie's eyes looked glazed and vacant, and her body shook so violently, he thought for a moment, she might be having a seizure.

Jake leaned down, getting as close to her as he possibly could, and held her tight. He could think of nothing else to do. So once again, he just held on.

It seemed strange to him how two strangers such as they, could be sharing such a personal moment. A week ago, the closest encounter he'd had with this woman was to help her carry in her groceries once, when he'd seen her struggling to balance her child on one hip and two bags on the other. Jake hadn't even known her daughter's name until the other night.

He drove Marnie home from the funeral when he didn't see a car in the parking lot, and thought maybe she'd taken the bus to get there. Ironically, she was staying in the same building he'd been relocated to.

Jake asked her what apartment number was now hers, but she didn't seem able to answer. He hadn't heard her make a sound yet—she hadn't spoken to anyone at the funeral, and hadn't even cried. *What should I do?* He picked up her purse, and she didn't make any move to stop him. Jake opened it and right on top was a set of keys. He flipped through them until he found one like the one he'd been given. Ah-ha! There it was. Apartment number 17.

He went around to the passenger side of the car and helped her out. She leaned heavily against him, and he wrapped his left arm around her to help hold her up. Slowly, they walked to her apartment. Jake opened the door and helped her inside, settling her on the couch in the small living room. His eyes glanced through the kitchen—there were no dishes, no food boxes sitting out. He wondered if she'd eaten at all. "Marnie? Marnie? Is there anything I can do for you? Are you hungry? Do you want something to drink?"

JUST HOLD ON

It didn't seem as if his words registered with her. He walked over and knelt down in front of her. Carefully, he took her face in his hands, and gently turned it upward so he could look directly into her eyes. It struck him that she just couldn't function right now.

He knew then, she needed someone to take care of her, as it appeared she didn't have anyone else. It became a struggle for him, because he didn't think he could take becoming emotionally involved with anyone again. He'd been alone for so long, and he kind of liked it that way. *But, maybe it's time. Maybe it's time to connect with somebody again.*

She certainly needed somebody. Marnie seemed so pitiful, so alone.

What if Cassie had found herself in a situation like this? He would want someone to take care of her—*Stop it, Jake, just stop it. No use in thinking about that.* But still…

He went to the kitchen and opened the refrigerator—nothing. The cabinets were empty. Had she really eaten nothing at all these past three days?

"Marnie? My apartment is just down the hall. I'm going to run back to my place and get some groceries. I'll make you dinner, okay? Is there anything special you'd like? I'm coming right back. Hear me? I'll be back in ten minutes. I'm not going to leave you alone."

Her vacant eyes just stared at the wall. It didn't seem like she even blinking at all.

He waited a second, then left. Rapidly, he strode down the hall to his place, opened the crate and took Barbossa out to relieve himself. Back inside, Jake scanned his cabinets. Admittedly, he didn't have a huge selection, but there were ingredients for spaghetti, and a loaf of garlic bread in the freezer. That would work. *I wonder what she likes to drink.* All he had was orange juice and a two liter of Coke, but it would have to do. It was better than nothing. The dog kept barking—he was hungry too, and he'd been in the crate since much earlier in the day. *Okay, okay...I guess I could take him back to her apartment.* He didn't think she would object.

CHAPTER TWO

Back at Marnie's place, he kicked the door open and carried in the groceries. "Marnie? Do you mind if I bring my dog in? It's okay if you don't want him here. I just thought, you know, he's been alone all day in his crate. He's real good, he shouldn't bother you."

Marnie didn't move. She just lay there, staring at the wall.

Jake went over and searched through the kitchen cabinets, looking for pots and pans,

Barbossa clambered up to Marnie, sliding up onto the couch with her and making himself very comfortable. Marnie didn't seem as if she cared, and she didn't object, so Jake left him there.

He found a pot and started the water boiling, and soon, his search yielded a cookie sheet to bake the garlic bread on. Jake often sang at home, when he was alone and cooking for himself, and he didn't realize he was even doing it—but he was. He'd been mostly fond of country music and eighties hits. Soon, the pasta had boiled and the garlic bread done. Next, he fixed her a plate and poured her a glass of Coke.

Jake felt proud of himself when he carried her dinner into the living room. "I hope you like spaghetti! I'm sorry, it was all I had on hand as I haven't had much time for shopping since—well, the other night. Want me to help you sit up? Marnie?"

She looked as limp as a ragdoll.

He sat the plate on the coffee table and put his hands around her waist—wow, she was so skinny! He sat her up and propped a pillow next to her, but she still wasn't responding. What should he do? She HAD to eat something, she seemed so dehydrated already.

Jake lifted the glass to her lips, and they parted automatically as he dumped the liquid in.

JUST HOLD ON

Reflexively, she swallowed. He repeated this maneuver, and thought he might have to do the same with the spaghetti. Wrapping a small bit around a fork, he fed her the pasta. She chewed mechanically, and he did it again.

After a few small bites, her eyes closed and she lay back down on the couch. *Okay,* Jake thought, *that's something, anyway.* He'd try again later. She did have a TV, so he turned that on then sat back on the couch, his hand automatically reaching for his dog.

Barbossa sighed contentedly and Jake gazed down at him, smiling. As he did, he caught a glimpse of Marnie's hands. They were a raw, bloody mess. Again, he felt waves of anger at a hospital staff that would send her home in such a condition. When things settled down, Jake thought he might just write a strongly worded letter of complaint to someone about that.

He went to the bathroom, found a washcloth and ran warm water on it. Back in the living room, Jake knelt in front of Marnie and gently took one of her small almost child-sized hands in his, wiping it as softly as he could, trying to remove the dried blood. In some places, he noticed the skin looked red, angry and felt kind of hot. Infected, maybe?

He needed something else, some kind of ointment or something. Jake didn't think he had anything like that back at the new place. Maybe, he could run out to the store later and pick some up. It was strange feeling this way, as if he wanted to take care of her, make her better. He hadn't felt this way in a long, long time. Being selfish was certainly easier, but this—this was something else. Something Jake just wasn't sure he was prepared for.

Jake wondered what he should do. It'd been four hours, and still Marnie hadn't moved or spoken. He stood up, sat back down. Stood up, paced a bit. Ran his hand through his hair. Wished he had a book, but his books were all burned up. The thought hurt his stomach a little, like all knotted up. The thick hard-cover fairytales he'd read to Cassie when she was little.

He shook his head. Should he leave Marnie there and go home? Should he stay here tonight? She hadn't asked him to, but then again, she didn't seem capable of asking for anything.

Maybe he would just stay tonight. It didn't seem like she should be left alone. He went back to the kitchen, washed up the dinner dishes, let the dog out again, fed him and made Marnie take a few sips of juice. She seemed to be asleep again, just now. He sat on the couch, drumming his fingers on the arm of it. "Marnie. Marnie." Jake patted her leg.

She opened her eyes.

"Will you be okay here, if I just run to the store really fast? I want to get you some groceries, and maybe something to put on your hands, so they don't get infected. Is that okay with you? Can I leave the dog here? That way, you won't be alone."

Blinking her eyes, she simply stared at him, but she didn't protest.

"I'm going to take your keys, okay? I don't want to leave you here alone with the door unlocked. I won't be gone long." Jake left in a hurry, feeling uncomfortable, leaving her in such an unstable condition.

Luckily, there was a small corner grocery store about ten minutes away. He grabbed a cart and started throwing in food. *Milk.* That would be good for her. *Orange juice.* He wasn't even sure what she liked, so he tried to get a variety. Some fruit. He stopped in the health section and found some antibiotic ointment.

What else might she need? Toilet paper. Soap. Shampoo—maybe he could help her wash and brush her hair. She would probably need a brush, too. He was back to her place in an hour.

She still hadn't moved.

Jake put away the stuff he'd bought, and took out the antibiotic ointment. Returning to the living room, he woke her up again, and told her what he was going to do. Rubbing the salve on her hands made him feel like he was taking good care of her.

She didn't resist; didn't even flinch as he rubbed it in, although he knew he must sting.

Jake looked around in the closets until he found a blanket for her. He brought it back and gently tucked it in around her small frame.

JUST HOLD ON

Barbossa had taken up residence in front of her, curled up in front of her stomach. It was sweet how the dog didn't even know this woman, but was so willing to lie beside her all day. Her own little three-legged guardian. Maybe he sensed she needed comfort.

Marnie lay there asleep. It was 1 o'clock in the morning, and he had no idea what to do. He felt tired, but he didn't want to go get into her bed. That just seemed kind of odd. Eventually, he slid down behind her on the couch, wrapping his arm around her and slipping himself under the blanket.

With as much as they'd had been through together in the last few days, doing that didn't seem as strange as it might have a week ago.

Marnie opened her eyes and actually glanced back at him, but she didn't ask him to leave. Laying her head back down, she slid her body a little closer to him.

Jake held her tight and they both fell asleep.

CHAPTER THREE

*I*t took him a moment when Jake first woke up the next day to realize where he was and what was going on. He pushed himself up on his elbow and rubbed his eyes in response to the light streaming in through the window. It'd been several years since he'd woken up in a home that wasn't his, holding a woman. He considered how that felt, and decided it wasn't so bad. Even though, these particular circumstances were just about the worst he could imagine, it wasn't such a terrible thing to wake up feeling so close to someone else. Feeling needed.

Jake took a moment to study her face, listen to her steady, even breathing. He was momentarily overwhelmed with a desire to brush his thumb against her soft white jaw and drop a kiss on her forehead—whoa! Where did that thought come from? Instead, Jake brushed some of the mass of matted hair from her face, and felt a strange kind of sharp pain catch in his chest.

Barbossa popped his head up too.

Jake hated to move Marnie at all; she looked peaceful for the first time in days, the pinched lines around her eyes and mouth finally relaxed. He didn't want the dog to have an accident in her apartment, though, so he shifted. Trying to slip himself out from his spot while sandwiched between Marnie's back and the couch, without disturbing her.

As soon as he moved, she clutched at him, sitting up quickly and gulping air, her eyes looked wild. Still holding his shirt, she started hyperventilating, sucking in breath after short, shallow breath. Her shoulders shook as she twisted the cotton of his T-shirt in her fist.

"It's okay, Marnie, it's okay. I'm here. I'm not leaving...I'm not leaving you. I'm right here. *Shhh*. I'm here, I'm here." Jake put his arms back around her, drawing her closer to him. "Breathe, honey, breathe. Calm down; *Shhh*."

To him, it sounded like she was choking. He put his hand on her forehead, stroking her hair. Slowly, he felt her start to relax, the rigid tension in her muscles melting just a bit.

He waited another ten minutes. "Okay, I'm going to get up now, okay? I'm just going to let the dog out, and get him some food. I'm not leaving. Hear me? I'm not leaving. I'm staying right here with you."

When he stood up, he watched her scramble backwards, and push herself up against the very back of the couch. Maybe it made her feel safer somehow.

Jake took Barbossa out, got his food and water, then poured Marnie and himself a glass of juice. He had to repeat the same motions as the day before, physically forcing her to sit up and pouring the juice into her mouth.

After just a few sips, she was too exhausted for any more and lay back down.

Jake thought if he went back out to the store, he should get her some chap-stick, her lips were so dry and cracked. He went back to the table and picked up the antibiotic ointment, and rubbed it all over her hands again.

It seemed like just these few activities had worn her out, as she curled up again and went back to sleep.

What should I do today? He should probably go home for a bit; call his boss and see when his next project would be due. Jake thought he could maybe get an extension on that, given the unusual circumstances of the week. He needed to go buy some clothes, since his were pretty much ruined in the fire. *I just really hate to leave Marnie here all alone.* She seemed so fragile. Maybe if he went fast at the store, he could get it all done in just a few hours. He could call his boss from her apartment and leave the dog there with her, so she didn't feel so alone.

Again, he was struck by the oddity of worrying about someone else. He hadn't had anyone in his life for several years. Now, he had a woman who was barely functioning and a three legged dog to care for. "Marnie. Marnie, wake up."

Sleepily, she opened her eyes and focused on him.

He wondered how much longer it would be before her pretty green eyes stopped looking so vacant and lifeless. "Marnie, listen. I need to go to the store, get a few things and sort out some stuff with my work. Can you stay here by yourself for a few hours?"

She looked a little panicked.

"Do you want me to leave the dog here? Or, would you rather I take him with me and let you rest?" He reached for the dog, who growled and showed Jake his teeth. *What the hell?* He'd never done that before—he always seemed like a very docile dog. He tried it again and again…the dog growled, deep and low.

Marnie reached out to Barbossa and looked Jake in the eye. She pulled the dog closer and Barbossa sprawled out in front of her, as if he were protecting her.

Jake shook his head. *Well then, I guess that settles that.*

JUST HOLD ON

He refilled the dog's dish, poured Marnie another glass of juice and put some fruit on a plate in case she got hungry while he was gone. He locked the door and went back to his place for a minute to get some cash.

Jake wondered about what store would probably be his best shot and decided the local mall would have just about everything he needed. His first stop was a men's store. He went in with a list already in his mind. He walked up to the salesgirl and told her the list he needed and that he would like to be out of the store in about fifteen minutes. She rushed off, saying that she could it in that time frame.

Next, he stopped at a shoe store and bought a pair of tennis shoes. He was making good time, and wondered if Marnie had any clothes.

She'd been wearing the same pair of jeans and that old T-shirt for a couple of days and probably hadn't been able to get any shopping done, what with the funeral and everything. Poor girl, this must all be very overwhelming for her.

He had enough money and he could help. Jake wandered into a store with girly looking items in the sales window, then realized he had no idea what to get for her. He knew he must've sounded very silly to the teenage salesgirl as he tried to approximate Marnie's size with his hands, holding them out in front of him in a slight circle, he thought might be about the size of her waist.

The girl peered at his hands and back up into his face, as if trying to decide if he was trying to pull some kind of joke on her.

"She's about this big around, I think? Then, maybe a couple inches taller than you. I need a few pair of jeans, some comfortable T-shirts, um, maybe some pajamas? Could you help me with that?"

Soon enough, he bought the clothes for Marnie while making a mental list of other things he wanted to buy for her. He wanted to get enough done to last a few days, because he didn't want to keep leaving her alone. He checked his watch—shoot, he'd already been gone two hours. He needed to go faster. He went to the electronics store and bought a laptop,

JUST HOLD ON

the first one he saw on sale. *Okay, that should be good.*

Driving back to the apartment building, he passed a McDonald's. *Maybe she'd like a milkshake.* So, he pulled in to the drive-thru. He wasn't sure what flavor to get, so he got chocolate. *Girls liked chocolate, right?*

Back at the apartment, he let himself in. He brought the clothes over to Marnie, surprised to see her awake.

"Look, I got you some stuff. I was thinking you probably didn't have any other clothes. I know I lost most of mine in the fire. I wasn't sure about your size, but the salesgirl helped me figure it out. I hope we were right. Do you like this?" He held up a shirt.

Marnie seemed to be looking at it, but it didn't seem like it was registering with her at all.

That's okay, she's just not ready to talk yet. Jake could wait. He brought her the milkshake, propped her up on a pillow in the corner of the couch. She lay there while he spooned it into her mouth. He didn't really mind doing it, as long as she was eating something.

"So, Marnie, listen. I was wondering if you'd like me to wash your hair? I know it probably bothers you, with the smell of smoke and everything. Um, I've never actually washed a woman's hair before. I'll try to be careful. What should we do? Do we just hang your head over the sink? I guess I could do that. Come on, I'll help you stand up. Do you think you can lean over the sink? Come on, Marnie, just take a few steps. I'll help you. Are there towels in the bathroom? I'll get one, just stand here. Lean against the counter if you need to."

Jake set it all up and then with a towel. "Okay, I'm back. Is the water warm enough? Okay, just put your head here, under the water." He felt like he was talking to a small child, but he didn't know how else to talk to her right now. "Marnie? Just tell me if I'm hurting you. I don't want to hurt you. Okay, the shampoo is in, let me just....Alright, now I'm just going to rinse it out and we're done. Wow, you have a LOT of hair, Marnie."

Jake listened to the sound of his own voice prattling on, and wondered why he felt compelled to

JUST HOLD ON

keep talking. He'd lived alone for many years, and never felt the need to talk to himself. Now, he couldn't stop talking to the dog, or to this woman who didn't seem to hear anything he said.

Marnie acted so worn out from having her hair washed that Jake wasn't sure she could walk all the way to the living room, so he scooped her up and carried her back to the couch. He positioned her, so her head rested on the arm of the couch, and her hair hung down over the side.

Wow, it'd been a really long time since he brushed a woman's hair. When his sister was young, he would sometimes help her brush out her long hair at night, then braid it so it wouldn't get tangled while she slept. He did just as he had with Cassie, his sister and started at the bottom, slowly brushing out the tangles in Marnie's auburn tresses. He felt so afraid of hurting her, he took just a tiny bit of hair in the brush each time.

Gradually, he worked up her hair until he finally had it all brushed out and straight. Jake remembered how easily his sister's hair would get knotted up if she slept with it wet. He should braid it or something. He looked around the apartment for something to tie her hair with, and in the bathroom, found an open package of rubber bands. *Perfect!* While he took two out, though, he recognized these bands from somewhere. Oh—Oh! These must have been the hair ties Marnie bought to braid Katie's hair for the funeral. That's where he remembered them from. Dark blue to match Katie's dress.

Well, there was nothing to do about it now. He didn't have a whole lot of options, and he didn't want to leave Marnie again, to run back out to the store. These would just have to do. He arched his back, trying to get the kinks out of it before he knelt back down to finish Marnie's hair. He'd been sitting there for over an hour, with his back hunched, brushing.

This time, he dragged one of the kitchen chairs over to the couch to sit on. Yes, much better. Slowly, deliberately, Jake began the process of braiding Marnie's long, thick hair. He was glad his fingers remembered how to braid. While he did, he started to hum, then sing. He hoped she liked country music.

JUST HOLD ON

CHAPTER FOUR

1 a.m. rolled around again. He sat there on the couch, Marnie curled up on the opposite end, the dog between them and wondered, not for the first time, what in the world he was doing. He couldn't stay here forever. He needed to rebuild his own life. He'd lost everything he owned in the fire.

Tomorrow, he would have to get the new laptop up and running and call his boss. Jake wondered too, about Marnie's life. *Why is she so alone? Why had no one come to the funeral for her little girl?* He felt really curious about Katie's father. Marnie didn't wear a wedding band, he noticed. Probably, just another jerk. Some guy who'd knocked her up and taken off long ago. He couldn't abide idiots like that.

How could a guy take advantage of such a sweet young woman? It made him so mad.

What about her parents? What could have happened between them for them not to come to their daughter during her darkest hours? He watched Marnie sleep, trying to make sense of the situation.

Maybe—maybe she'd run away when she was younger. Maybe *The Jerk guy* talked her into it, and she followed him, believing he would love her and care for her. Maybe, she'd been afraid to tell her parents she'd gotten pregnant. The longer he thought about it, the more it seemed to make sense to him. Maybe her parents never even knew she had a baby. The Jerk probably cut off her ties to her family and now, she didn't know how to go back.

Jake wanted to punch this guy, then run him over with a truck. He thought about the situation. Maybe once Marnie was doing better, he could help her reconnect with her parents. She should have her family around her at a time like this.

Jake then thought about his own parents. His dad left eleven years ago. Just walked right out on him and his mom, right after his sister's funeral.

JUST HOLD ON

Right, when they both needed him the most. They'd never heard from him again. His poor mom. The strain of losing her daughter, then her husband in such short succession really messed her up. It seemed like she just lost her hold on reality. She'd never been a very strong person. Now, she lived in a home, about a half an hour away from him and he visited twice a month. The doctors said she wouldn't get better, and after so long, he tended to believe them.

The Jerk who'd walked out on Marnie was probably just like Jake's idiot dad. He wished he knew where The Jerk was; he'd like to go pay him a visit.

Jake thought back to the night of the fire. It'd been so frightening—the smell of the smoke—Marnie and Katie. The throngs of people outside, crying and yelling, the wailing of the ambulance sirens. Disorder everywhere. It was funny how strange your thoughts become in the middle of a crisis.

Jake always believed he would know just what to do if something like that happened, but then—

when it did, he felt like he couldn't think straight at all. He felt glad, though, that he hadn't forgotten the dog. Barbossa had really been a comfort to Marnie. She could barely stand to let go of him for more than a minute. He guessed, if he was honest…the dog kind of comforted him, too.

Tomorrow, he would have to get Marnie to eat more. It worried him, seeing her like this. *Am I doing something wrong, or just not doing enough?* His tired eyes were red and itchy, so he kept rubbing at them. Same as he had the night before, he slipped down behind Marnie on the couch, pulling the blanket over him.

In her sleep, she scooted back into his arms as he settled his around her.

The dog then stood up, went around in a few circles, then hunkered back down into the space in front of Marnie's belly.

The three of them slept that way until early the next afternoon.

~***~

JUST HOLD ON

Looking at his watch, Jake couldn't believe how long he'd slept. Oh, his leg hurt so much. He reached down to rub it. In a few more days, he would need to go and get the stitches out. He shifted his weight.

Marnie bolted upright, blindly reaching out to clutch at him. Holding part of his shirt balled up in her hand, she stared up at him frantically, panting.

His heart pitied her. She felt so scared of being left alone. He guessed, he could lay there with her for a few more minutes. It wasn't like he had anyplace else to go.

An hour later, he stood, stretching. Sleeping on the couch with another adult and a dog was really screwing with his back, but the couch seemed like the only place Marnie could get comfortable, so he didn't want to mess that up.

He let the dog out, and went to the kitchen to see what he could make for breakfast. *Omelets!* Very good for her, some protein. He'd gotten used to where everything was in her kitchen, quickly locating the pans and utensils he would need. While he cooked, he started to sing. Banging the spatula on the countertop, he belted out, "Bow, bow, ba-bow. Bow, bow, ba-bow. Hmm…Sweet home Alabama…"

He wished Marnie would talk to him and he wondered how long it would be before she did. He'd become used to silence at his place, but here…having another person in such close proximity, it became kind of uncomfortable to be the only one making any noise.

Marnie as usual, lay there unmoving, as he carried the plate of food to her.

He sat her up again, cutting into the food to feed her small bites. "So, do you want to try on your new clothes? I hope they fit. Marnie? Do you want me to help you? Here, I'll pull off the tags. Okay—do you want me to go out, give you some privacy?"

She sat, staring at him. Her heavy eyelids fluttered with exhaustion.

Okay, I can do this. It doesn't have to be weird. We're both adults here. Wasn't like he'd never seen a naked woman before, although it'd been quite some time since he had. He rolled the bottom of the filthy torn T-shirt she wore up a bit, and waited a minute. She didn't protest, so he took that as a sign to continue.

Averting his gaze, he gazed at the floor as he pulled the shirt up over her head and grabbed the new one off the floor, slipping it onto her. The jeans might prove to be a little bit trickier. He tried just to be businesslike, getting it done quickly, not looking, just slipping off the old ones and yanking the new ones up onto her slight frame.

Great. So, she was dressed in clean clothes, her hair was still in the braid he put it in the night before, and she'd eaten some. *It's all good... yes, good.* He remembered to put some more ointment on her hands, which were finally starting to look a little better—the angry red edges of the splits in her skin beginning to heal.

Jake led her to the bathroom again, and nudged her in like he'd done quite a few times now, then waited for her to be done.

Marnie looked exhausted from the morning already, so he tucked her back into her spot on the couch and let her rest more.

VALARIE SAVAGE KINNEY

It bothered him, the way she would just stare at the bare wall. He wondered if he could move the entertainment center with the TV on it. At least then, she could stare at something different. Jake shoved it, went around to the other side and pulled on it, until finally it was in place, covering the space her eyes were focused on. *There, that's better.* At least, it made him feel better.

Maybe tonight, he would rent some movies to watch. He wondered too, if she liked books. Jake always had. He loved to get lost in a good read. Maybe he could go to the library, check some books out and read them to her. He wanted so badly to reach her, to see some life in her eyes. Hear her voice.

Jake thought back to when he'd been with Alexis. *How long had it been? Ten years? Yes—wow.* He hadn't realized it'd been so long. Poor Alexis...he really treated her badly. It wasn't her fault, the problems he had at the time. She was a good woman, but at the time, he'd been really messed up. It was better for her to be without him.

JUST HOLD ON

He would've been a burden to her—but if he were truthful with himself, she'd been a burden to him.

Jake cared about her a lot. He even thought at one time, he loved her, but love became a burden. He learned that much. He loved his father, and the pain of losing him was a terrible load. He'd loved his little sister too, and when Cassie died, right in front of him, he thought the weight of that pain would kill him. He really did. And his poor mom? She loved her little family, and it all disintegrated so rapidly.

Jake felt helpless as he watched the burden of her love and the pain it brought, destroy her mind. As far as he could see, it was better not to care at all, rather than to care so much and end up hurt that way.

So, he'd made some decisions. Maybe they were right, maybe not. It felt like the right thing to do at the time. Once it was clear his dad wasn't coming back, then once the doctors sat Jake down and told him his mother needed to be in a facility with around-the-clock care, he decided to be done with these awful emotions.

VALARIE SAVAGE KINNEY

He then resigned from his teaching job at the local middle school, being around all the kids and Cassie's friends, just hurt him all the more. Besides, the very nature of teaching meant he needed to interact with people: colleagues, students, parents. It all became too much.

Quitting his job had been just the beginning. Soon, he stopped returning phone calls from friends. At first, it was difficult because he hated to hurt their feelings, but after a while, it became easier. He disconnected his home phone and quit going out, except for the necessities. Jake then found a new job, freelancing articles for a magazine. Mostly, he worked from home after that and hardly ever needed to go in to the office. The smaller his world became, the happier he thought he was.

The final tie to cut was with Alexis. She'd been supportive through Cassie's death and Jake's dad's departure, spending hours sitting with his mother. She held him at night through the worst of his grief, staying up with him when the nightmares begun, trying to calm him when the anxiety attacks started.

JUST HOLD ON

She was a good woman, but he didn't feel like a good man.

Jake decided it would be better just to end the relationship then. He thought it would probably end anyway, because Alexis would eventually, get sick and tired of his moping and staying in the house. Then, she would want to break it off. He thought it would be easier to get it over with…deal with all the loss at once. *She was so hurt by it.*

He still remembered her face when he told her it was over. She cried, begged and made promises, but he'd been resolute. Jake didn't want to care about anybody else. He didn't want to worry about anyone else—and he most certainly no longer wanted to be burdened with love.

Jake let out a half-hearted laugh. Ten years. When he was a younger man…not that he was old now at 35, but he certainly wasn't young. He would have thought he would die from going ten years without sex. Apparently, celibacy wasn't terminal, especially he guessed, if it was self-imposed. He reflected on his life since telling Alexis, "Goodbye."

VALARIE SAVAGE KINNEY

He didn't think he'd been miserable. He stayed home a lot and didn't really have any friends, visited his mom at the home twice a month. He watched a lot of crime dramas on TV, and was fond of movies with Geoffrey Rush in them. He felt healthy. Paid well for his work and had been able to save a good amount over the years.

It wasn't a terrible life, but it was getting kind of lonely. That'd been part of the reason he got the dog. *A dog*, he decided, *would be another presence in his home*. He'd chosen a rescue dog, because it made him feel like he was doing some good in the world. A dog is something to care about, but not to love and Jake didn't think it would crush him if he lost the dog someday—though it seemed like he was getting too fond of the stupid mutt already.

Jake wished he knew how to get in contact with Marnie's parents. They probably really missed her, and he wondered how long it'd been since she'd seen them last. Katie had been about two years old, certainly not more than three. A shame her parents had never known the child…she'd been adorable.

JUST HOLD ON

He could picture Katie in his mind, the day he helped Marnie with her groceries. Her thumb in her mouth that day, and it had been windy. Her wispy blond hair blowing all over the place, and her green eyes—so like her mother's—watched him curiously as he jogged across the parking lot and offered to help Marnie get her things carried in.

In an instant, the image was replaced by one of Katie trapped in her crib, the night of the fire. Jake tried so hard to save her. He'd wanted nothing more in the world, than for the CPR to work and make her chest start rising on its own. He wondered if she'd already been dead even as they struggled to free her from the baby bed. He thought for sure he'd felt a pulse once they were outside, but maybe it'd been his imagination.

The tragedy became a terrible reminder of the day Cassie died. He performed CPR on her too, and failed Cassie just the same way he failed Katie. He didn't want to fail Marnie any more than he already had, and felt determined to do anything humanly possible to help her get better.

CHAPTER FIVE

Marnie needed a bath or a shower, but Jake didn't think she would be able to stand up long enough to take one on her own. He'd been considering this for a few days, trying to think of a way to help her without compromising her modesty. He didn't want her to think he was taking advantage of her, but it'd been days since the fire, and she still smelled like smoke when he held her. He thought it would make her feel better too, a nice hot bath.

Washing her hair helped, and he did that a couple times a week, but she hadn't had a bath since before the fire, and he was determined to get this done somehow.

Jake went to the bathroom and started drawing a hot bath, wishing he had thought to buy some bubble bath. Girls liked that sort of thing…didn't they? *Hey! Dish soap makes bubbles. I could dump some of that in.* He wanted her to enjoy it, so he poured in a lot of soap, then left to go explain to her what they were going to do.

Still, just that empty vacant stare.

"Okay, Marnie, so we're going to get you into the bathtub. I've got a nice, hot bubble bath waiting for you. Won't that feel nice?" He stood her up and helped her walk to the bathroom.

Oh...Maybe he had put in a touch too much soap...there were a LOT of bubbles. *Crap. Um...* He tried to think.

"Okay, okay, well I guess I'm the dumb one here, huh? This might be a funny story one day, Marnie. Okay, let's sit you here on the toilet, and I'll get—I guess I'll fetch a bowl and start getting some of these bubbles out of here. Wow, I can't believe I did something so stupid! Oh well, I guess it's nothing too terrible."

Jake bailed and bailed and bailed those bubbles, and after a few minutes, he started to sing. It seemed like such a ridiculous situation, he may as well keep making it more ridiculous, so he started singing

AC/DC's *You Shook Me All Night Long* to Marnie, as he got the bubbles down to a decent level.

Next, he decided to do what had to be done the same way he got her dressed every day. Briskly and efficiently, he pulled off her clothes, looking at the ceiling as he did so. Wrapping one arm under her knees and the other behind her head, he gently laid her down in the bathtub where she sank into the water like a dead weight. Taking a washcloth, and trying—*trying very hard*—not to think about what he was doing, he washed her body while keeping his thoughts busy on anything else. Baseball, the latest episode of NCIS, what to make for dinner. *Whew, this was difficult.*

He figured while he was at it, he may as well wash her hair again. Bracing his hand behind her head, he guided it down to the brink of the water to wet it, and poured in the shampoo. *Okay,* he thought, *this wasn't the brightest idea either*. He couldn't rinse her hair in the water which was filled with dish soap bubbles. He leaned back to grab the bowl he used for bubble bailing, turned the faucet back on and started to rinse her hair with the fresh water, not realizing until it was too late that running more water into the tub was going to create more bubbles.

Jake now felt glad he stuck to five minute showers himself.

He lifted her head up to start drying her hair with a towel and she came up, half sitting, in the water. Wow. Her face, and neck, and shoulders—they were so—*wet*. She looked so pretty and—and very wet, there in the water. *Wow. It is really hot in here.* Jake's throat felt dry and he hadn't realized she would be getting so *wet* in the bathtub.

He hadn't thought this through very well at all. He blinked, shook his head, then stared at the ceiling. *Baseball, NCIS, dinner. Baseball, NCIS, dinner. Okay*...he took a deep breath. He could do this.

Finally, they were done with the bathing part. Jake reached down and pulled the drain in the tub to let the water out, and as it started to drain, he wrapped a towel over Marnie to cover her. He grabbed another towel to dry her with, very quickly.

Okay, okay, on with her clothes. Then—they were done. Jake carried Marnie back out to the couch and settled her into her blankets.

He thought now might be a good time for one of his five-minute showers. A. Very. Cold One.

Well, Marnie and the dog were sleeping again. Now, would probably be a good time to take care of work, so Jake called his boss and talked to him for a bit. He told him he lost what he'd been working on before the fire and, although he purchased a new laptop, he would need some extra time to finish the assignment.

Jake felt thankful his boss was an understanding guy. *Two extra weeks. Great!* In two weeks, he felt sure Marnie would be getting back on her feet and he would be able to get caught up on work.

CHAPTER SIX

Two weeks. Jake could hardly believe two weeks had passed, and not much changed. Every night, Jake slept beside Marnie on the couch, the dog curled up somewhere near them. Each morning, when he woke and started to move, Marnie would panic and bolt upright, breathing heavily, clutching him. He would reassure her he wasn't going anywhere, and lay back down with her, holding her until her breathing became more normal and he could feel her body relax.

Sometimes, it took twenty minutes…sometimes it would be an hour, sometimes longer. Then, he would get up, stretch, tend to the dog, make her breakfast and feed it to her.

Some days, Jake worked half-heartedly on his assignment. Marnie still hadn't spoken…still hadn't cried. He felt pretty sure this wasn't normal grief and realized, he might need some help with her. He rarely even went back to his apartment anymore. Jake wondered if he may as well give up his lease and just move in with Marnie for the time being. He already basically lived here.

Occasionally, he thought he might be giving people the wrong idea about them, and he hoped Marnie didn't worry about that. If asked, he would tell people the truth, but nobody ever asked him. They weren't sleeping together. Well, he corrected that thought—they *were sleeping* together, but only very literally. He smiled at the idea.

Inexplicably, he then found himself looking forward to the time each night when he would slip in behind Marnie, his arms around her and feel her snuggle back into him. Sometimes, she would push back against him so hard, it was as if she were trying to get inside him.

How ever they ended up, Barbossa would wait for them to get settled, then circle around a bit and sprawl out in front of Marnie. Jake had forgotten how nice it could be to feel this close to someone, holding her tight and listening to her regular breathing.

"Marnie? I was thinking. Look, I know we aren't together or anything, but it seems like I'm here so much, I was wondering if I should just give up my lease. Then, I could pay the rent here, so you don't have to worry about coming up with that money. I mean, I wouldn't tell people—not that I talk to many people really—but I'm not going to tell people that we're dating or anything. I don't want to give a bad impression. Not that it's really anybody's business, anyway, what we do. Not that we're doing anything—I mean, not anything wrong. Well, you know what I mean. I hope? I just thought it might be easier on you. So, you know, I don't have to leave as much, and you won't have to worry about the rent or light bills. I can take care of that. It's not a problem. What do you think? Marnie? I wish you would talk to me. I'd like to hear your voice." Jake watched her.

Nothing. She stared at the TV while time ticked by. He'd taken to leaving it on constantly, because it made him feel better to think that she was looking at something at least. Plus, the TV made some noise in the otherwise overly quiet apartment. He wished he knew what she might be thinking. Actually, he wondered if she was thinking at all. If anything was even going on in her mind.

Twenty minutes later, he felt Marnie move and peered down at her. She was reaching her hand toward him; it was the first time she'd ever made a move to touch him. Jake watched, as her hand moved slowly across the couch, finally lacing her fingers into his. He took his other hand and placed it on top of their joined hands.

Her hand still looked raw in places and scabbed over in others, but gazing at her hand in his, he thought it was a beautiful sight. Jake stared into her eyes. They were focused on him for a change, and he knew then—she'd been paying attention to what he just said.

"Marnie? What do you think? Do you want me to stay here? At least for now—I can always look for another apartment once you get back on your feet. I promise…Marnie, I just want you to know I don't want to take advantage of you. I hope you don't think that about me. I'm not looking to get anything from you. I don't expect anything from you. You're the first woman I've been this close to in ten years. I—I think I feel so close to you, because we went through such a terrible time together. I feel like you're the only one who can understand what we went through that night. I know we haven't known each other very long, but I care about you, Marnie, and I want to try to help you get better. I really—I care about you. So, should I call the landlord, and bring my stuff over? I don't have much."

    Jake suddenly realized how badly he wanted to hear her say yes. He wanted to hear her voice ask him to stay and take care of her.

    She still didn't speak, but after a moment she looked directly into his eyes and it seemed like she was trying to convey something to him. Then, he felt her squeeze his hand tightly. His heart soared. God, she has such beautiful green eyes.

~***~

VALARIE SAVAGE KINNEY

It didn't take long for Jake to get his things moved in. Pretty much, all he had were the things he purchased since the fire. None of the furniture there was his, so he only fetched a couple of bags.

Three weeks had gone by, and they'd technically been living together for one whole week. Jake never lived with a woman before. He'd thought about asking Alexis to move in with him, years ago when they were together, but then his sister died and everything suddenly went downhill. Jake kind of liked it now. He liked hurrying home when he was out, knowing Marnie was there waiting for him to get back. He liked picking up little things for her, hoping to make her smile. Almost every time he went out, he would stop at McDonald's and bring her back a chocolate milkshake. He still had to feed her everything she ate; she just wasn't strong enough yet to be able to do it herself. It was becoming so routine to him he'd almost forgotten how abnormal the whole situation really was.

JUST HOLD ON

Jake became more determined by the day to make Marnie respond to him somehow. Sometimes, he felt like he wanted to make her really mad about something, just to see if she would liven up and yell at him. He would've have been so grateful just to hear her scream!

He knew he needed to do it, but he didn't want to explain to Marnie about his mother. He thought it would be even more depressing for her. To be honest, it was depressing for him to talk about. He felt afraid the discussion might spin from his mom to Cassie, and he didn't want that. However, Jake felt guilty for not visiting his mom and knew he needed to go see her.

One day, after Marnie had been cleaned up and fed, after he brushed and re-braided her hair, he told her he had some errands to run. He knew she hated it when he left, but he was never gone long, and she did have Barbossa to hold until he came back.

Jake drove to the home his mother lived in. It was a nice place, as far as places like that went. An old, rambling farmhouse, set a little ways outside the town on a nice plot of land. The residents could go outside throughout the day for fresh air, and Jake wondered if his mother ever did that. He didn't knock, just walked in.

The nurse smiled when she saw him. "Jake! We haven't seen you around in a while! How nice to see you. Your mother will be so happy you're here!"

He knew that wasn't quite true. His mother didn't even remember his name half the time. His mom was sitting up in the living room, in a rocking chair. She looked so old and fragile. He remembered the way she used to dress, back before Cassie died. She would always be dressing up for some reason or other, and wearing pretty jewelry. He hated the way they dressed her here, in fleece jogging suits—he could swear, she wore the same exact outfit every day, just a different color.

"Hi, mom!" Jake called brightly as he bent in to hug her. He sat across from her in a chair and took her hands in his. "Mom? It's me, Mom…it's Jake. How've you been?"

She smiled faintly while looking a bit confused, as if she realized she was supposed to know who he was and why he was there. He hadn't told her about the fire, or about Marnie, because he didn't want to upset her. Jake spent an hour with his mom, and felt like he was really starting to tire of one-sided conversations. His mother, Marnie, the dog—he wanted someone to talk back to him, someone to be interested in what he had to say and how he felt.

Jake went to find the nurse to let her know he was getting ready to leave. On a whim, he asked the nurse if he could talk to her for a few minutes. Without giving away too much information, he explained how he had a friend who'd recently been through a traumatic experience and now didn't seem to be able to speak.

After listening for a while, the nurse suggested how maybe Jake's friend could communicate through another avenue, such as writing in a notebook, and suggested he make sure she was seeing a doctor.

Jake stopped on the way home to pick up a notebook and some pens, but he didn't understand what seeing a doctor could do for Marnie. She was depressed, and understandably so. She'd been through pretty much the most horrifying experience a mother could go through. A doctor couldn't change that, and Jake didn't think pills would do anything for her. His mother took all kinds of pills and he'd never seen her get better. If anything, she seemed worse off. Time was what Marnie needed, time and care, but he thought the notebook was a good idea.

CHAPTER SEVEN

Marnie was sleeping again, and Jake felt truly bored. He wandered around the apartment, looking for something to do. It was funny, he'd been basically living here for over a month, and he had never been to the bedroom. It wasn't like it was really *her* bedroom. He didn't think she'd ever even slept in the bed. She hadn't decorated the room either, but somehow, he felt like he was doing something naughty when he turned the knob and stepped in.

The bedroom looked a whole lot like the bedroom in the apartment he'd been staying in before. Very plain with full sized bed covered in a plain blue comforter. White vertical blinds at the window, a small white chest of drawers in the corner. Wait—what was that box?

A large blue tub with a lid sat near the closet. He stepped closer and lifted the lid. A box of photo albums—where did this come from? The previous tenant? Surely, they would have cleaned the place out before they rented it again.

Curious, he stepped closer and lifted the lid, taking out an album. This was an album full of pictures of Katie! How had this box escaped the fire? He thought about this for a while. Of course, Marnie and Katie had just moved in a couple weeks before the fire, maybe Marnie put her things in storage somewhere and hadn't gotten all of it out yet.

Leaning against the bed, he pulled the box nearer to him and started looking through the albums. He didn't think Marnie would mind, they were just about as close as two people could be by now.

The first book was all Katie, starting with Marnie and the baby in the hospital. Marnie looked so tired in the picture, but proud as she held the tiny,

JUST HOLD ON

wrinkled newborn on her chest. Her eyes actually looked like they were sparkling, and Jake thought to himself that he would do just about anything to make her eyes look like that again. Marnie was really a very beautiful woman. It was difficult not to notice that. It wasn't like he had any plans for—anything, but he was a man, she was a beautiful woman, and he just—noticed.

Jake laughed, he'd been celibate for ten years, so he guessed he could survive living with a woman like Marnie and not try to get her into bed. He might be the *only* man who could. He laughed again. *I am living a very odd life right now.*

The next page of the album startled him. There was a young man in the photo, leaning down, so his head came level with Marnie's, his hand resting on the newborn she held, and he was smiling so wide, he looked like an advertisement for some kind of tooth whitener. Jake noticed the guy had light blond hair, just like Katie's had been. That must have been where she got it from. So, THIS was The Jerk?

He didn't look like a jerk in the pictures, but you never could tell. Apparently, he must have led

Marnie on, and left after the baby was born. How cold hearted could the guy be? Jake flipped through the pages, watching Katie grow from a tiny newborn to a slightly older baby, learning to hold her head up and smile, then to a bigger baby learning to crawl.

Marnie must have taken pictures all day long, day after day, to get this many. It became painfully obvious to Jake how very proud she was of her little girl. Katie's first birthday—he could tell because she had a little pink birthday hat on and cake smeared all over her face, grinning at the camera with one big tooth in her mouth. Katie opening presents on her birthday, with Marnie sitting beside her, helping her tear the wrapping paper off.

Wait a minute—there was that guy again, Katie's dad—he had to be her dad. So, he must have come around some. That was good, maybe he wasn't the idiot Jake assumed he was. But if he wasn't, why hadn't he shown up at his child's funeral? What kind of father didn't show up at something that important?

Jake put the photo album back in the box, and went out to check on Marnie and Barbossa. She was

JUST HOLD ON

still sleeping, her arm wrapped securely around the dog, so he went back to the bedroom and pulled out another album. The first page hit him like a ton of bricks. It was a wedding album. A wedding album with pictures of Marnie and the guy in the baby's photos.

Marnie had been *married*? He hadn't expected this. Of course, he hadn't known her very well before the fire, but she hadn't ever worn a ring that he had noticed. Jake hadn't seen the guy around the old building at all—had he left her? They couldn't have been married very long. Jake didn't think Marnie was older than 23, maybe 24. They looked so happy in these wedding photos, acting silly and posing.

One picture in particular was so…perfect. The guy, who looked taller than Marnie, was looking down at her and Marnie had her face tipped up toward his. Her veil covered the auburn hair that hung in curls to her waist and she looked so indescribably happy.

Jake felt his eyes tear up. What had happened?

VALARIE SAVAGE KINNEY

He flipped through some more pages and it looked like they'd been really happy. It was a little hard for him to accept the notion of how she'd been married. In his mind, he made up a story which pegged her as a young struggling single mother, left alone by some jerk boyfriend.

He really had it all wrong. It looked like they'd gotten married before the baby came, so it wasn't like they thought they had to get married. He couldn't imagine why the guy would have left Marnie and the baby.

Jake kept flipping through the albums. He opened the next one and his hands started to shake. These were photos of Marnie and the guy—her husband—at some kind of military ceremony. He was in full uniform; she was all dressed up in a green dress. *Was this a graduation ceremony? Had her husband been in the service?* He wished he could ask her these questions, but he didn't dare. He kept looking.

Toward the end of the album, there was a letter pressed in between two of the pages. Jake started to open it, then thought maybe he shouldn't. Curiosity

JUST HOLD ON

won out, however, and he pulled the letter from the album.

Dear Mrs. Sanders,
We regret to inform you—

Jake took a deep breath. *Stop, stop this right now. I don't want to know this...I don't want to see this,*

—Your husband, Lieutenant Daniel Sanders...killed in the line of duty, serving his country...

Hastily, Jake folded the letter and put it back where he'd gotten it, slammed the lid down on the box and sat there looking at it. The letter was dated six months ago. Her husband hadn't left her—he was dead. Jake tried to wrap his mind around this news. *Oh,* he thought, *oh, Marnie.* No wonder she's so lost in grief. Her husband died, and now her daughter was dead too.

Jake's heart ached for this poor woman. He wanted so badly to make things better for her. For the first time in many years, Jake wept. Not silently with tears rolling down his cheeks, but loudly, with great racking sobs that shook his very core. His chest hurt and he lay down on the bed. Once he started, he couldn't stop weeping.

He wanted, *needed* someone. There was so much awfulness—everywhere. Cassie, his father, his mother, Marnie, little Katie and the fire. *So much pain.* He was tired of dealing with the pain all by himself.

Wiping his eyes, he stumbled out to the living room, shutting the bedroom door behind him. "Marnie? Marnie?" Jake climbed onto the couch behind her, wrapping his arms around her the way he usually did before they went to sleep at night.

Marnie looked concerned, confused.

He knew he was still crying, he could feel the tears falling down his face, but was powerless to stop. He wanted something to take the pain away. He held her so tight, his face pressed hard against her hair, his body shaking with sobs.

JUST HOLD ON

For a change, and for the first time, she turned to him and wrapped her arms around him, holding him close to her chest.

She still couldn't seem to speak, but she knew he was hurting too, and she wanted to give him some comfort. Marnie pressed a gentle kiss to the top of his head, then rested her chin there, and they stayed that way until morning.

CHAPTER EIGHT

After that night, Jake felt closer to Marnie than ever. He actually thought he felt closer to her than he ever did with Alexis. It seemed strange, when he thought about it, because he thought sex was supposed to bring two people as close as they could be. He'd slept with Alexis for two years, and never had with Marnie, but he still felt much, much closer to her.

He thought he might tell Marnie about Alexis sometime. *Later.* He wondered if Marnie would ever tell him about her husband—Daniel.

It'd been six weeks. Six weeks, and still Marnie hadn't spoken…hadn't cried…hadn't used the notebook he'd given her to communicate with. But her hands had healed up, and it looked like she maybe gained a pound or two. Her lips were no

JUST HOLD ON

longer so cracked and dry, and sometimes, she sat up on the couch by herself.

Jake felt like she was making progress, just very slowly.

One night, as they were sleeping on the couch, Jake felt Marnie start to shake. It reminded him of the way she trembled during Katie's funeral and he woke instantly, wondering what was wrong. He studied her, and saw she was still asleep.

She thrashed around on the couch, twisting the blanket around herself, her eyes open but not awake, drenched in sweat. It looked like she might be having a nightmare.

Jake wasn't sure what to do—he'd always heard not to wake up a sleepwalker, but she wasn't really sleepwalking. He held her shoulder, tapping it gently. "Marnie? Marnie, wake up. It's a nightmare, Marnie...wake up! Can you hear me? It's Jake. Wake up!"

Breathing hard and fast, she blinked. She looked at him, and he felt like he could see her heart through her eyes. It was broken into pieces. Marnie gulped air like she'd been drowning, then leaned over the couch and threw up.

Jake held her tight, pulling her hair away from the mess. "It's okay, it's okay. I'll clean it up. It's okay, honey." He couldn't believe how hard her stomach was heaving. She surely didn't eat much, but he could feel so much force wrenching her body.

Once it was over, he cleaned up the mess, then brought a cloth to wipe her face. She looked so little, so spent, curled up on the couch. She was still breathing hard, and her bangs were wet with sweat. Jake lifted her up and sat beneath her, bringing her head back down, so that it lay on his lap. He bent and kissed her forehead, stroking her hair from her face with his hand.

Hours passed. He started to doze off while sitting up when he heard a strange sound—a whisper.

Jake gazed down.

Marnie was staring at him, her lips moving. Her voice came out faint, and he bent his ear down to hear what she was saying.

It was only one word. "Daniel..."

JUST HOLD ON

Jake's heart broke for her all over again, and he now felt so relieved he knew who Daniel had been. He lifted her up a little closer and started to rock her gently, slowly, back and forth, the way he had done when Cassie was little and had a scary dream. Back then, he could tell Cassie to not be scared—the monsters weren't real—nothing bad was going to happen to her. He wished he could say the same to Marnie, but he knew he couldn't.

It seemed like that night became a turning point for both of them. The next day, Jake told Marnie he'd found the box with the photos, and had looked through them.

Her gaze held his for a few minutes, then darted back to the TV. She knew that he knew, and it was enough. Jake sometimes thought he saw something in her eyes, like she'd become a little more aware. They didn't look quite as vacant as they had over the last seven weeks, and it occurred to him if she was starting to wake up, she might need a little more to occupy her mind. She was probably getting sick of watching TV all day, every day, so he went to the local library and stocked up on several good, thick books. He picked books of almost every genre: fiction, non-fiction, sci-fi, even a few dog books. Nothing heavy though, he didn't want to read anything upsetting to her. He focused on stuff that looked funny, or had a happy ending.

That night, Jake sat down and turned the TV volume down with the remote.

Marnie stared at him, questioning what was changing their little routine, and he held up a book. "I thought I'd read to you. Do you like books? I've always loved to read, though I haven't much lately. This is a book about dog agility, it's called 'Dogged Pursuit'. I thought maybe we'd learn something we could teach Barbossa. I've never really considered doing dog agility with him, but I don't know…maybe this book will convince me it would be fun. I wonder if there are agility classes for special needs dogs like him. Could he do agility with only three legs? What do you think?"

As usual, she didn't respond, just stared at him, unblinking.

He slid his glasses down his nose a bit, and began to read. It turned out to be rather a funny book. The author was pretty clever and a few times, Jake laughed right out loud. He wondered what Marnie's laugh sounded like and whether—he would ever hear it.

Once he'd read for about an hour his throat started getting dry, so he stopped. He noticed she'd been watching him the whole time. It felt good to know he had her attention, even if just for a little while. Tomorrow, maybe, he would read to her some more, since she seemed to like it.

It struck him that, as little as he'd been outside in the last seven weeks, she hadn't been out at all. *Seven weeks was almost two months! Had it really been that long? Strange.* It seemed like each day melted into the next. Half the time, he wasn't even sure which day of the week it was.

He'd taken on shorter, lighter assignments at work, saying he was still very stressed from the fire, and that was working out well for him. He had quite a good amount of money tucked away in the bank, and he was making enough each month to afford the rent on the apartment.

Marnie really should get out though, he thought. It couldn't be healthy for her not to be out in the sunshine. It was cold out, with a couple inches of snow on the ground, but there was still sunshine. Where could he take her? *The park, maybe?*

"Marnie? Hey, do you think you'd like to get out of here for a little while? It's supposed to be nice out tomorrow…up in the forties with sun. Would you like to go for a car ride, or maybe go to the park?"

Her head whipped up, eyes looking frightened.

Okay, maybe it would be too much for her. Besides, he didn't think she even owned a coat. He should go buy her one—yes, that's what he would do. Give her a little more time and meanwhile, he would buy her a nice, warm coat. He didn't want her to get cold. "Okay honey, if you aren't ready, that's all right. We'll just stay in. Someday, probably someday soon, you're going to have to get out a little bit though. You don't have to be around other people, but you need fresh air and sunshine. I don't want you to get sick on me."

JUST HOLD ON

Seemingly reassured, Marnie curled up into her blankets.

"So—I have something else to talk to you about, Marnie." Jake climbed up onto the opposite end of the couch, propping her legs on his lap and putting his hands on top of them. It was a way they often sat together. "Did you know it's been seven weeks? I was thinking of that today. Seven weeks, Marnie. It's hard to believe, isn't it? I was wondering—I mean, I know—well, to be honest, I'm not as young as you are Marnie, and this sleeping on the couch every night? Well, as much as I really love holding you, you know, the way we do—this sleeping on the couch every night is really killing my back. Um—so I was thinking, you've got a bed, and it's a lot bigger than this couch. So, would you have a problem with us starting to sleep in there?"

Marnie was indeed listening, he could tell. She turned her face toward him, just looking at him.

He waited a few beats.

"Well, what do you think? Look—I hope you know me well enough by now, Marnie, to know I'm not looking to—you know. I'm not looking to take advantage of you. I'm not going to try anything in there, any more than I've tried anything out here…"

He then, waited a few more beats.

"I mean—I really do care about you, Marnie, and I don't want to screw up our friendship. You mean a lot to me. This—us, the way we are right now, that's fine with me. It's enough. Being together with you every day and holding you at night, it means a lot. It's more than I've had with anybody in a long, long time. I don't want that to change—I just thought, maybe, if we're going to be together like this for a while, then at least in the bed, we could stretch out a little bit. We can bring the dog too, if you want."

Marnie looked as if she were considering it for a few minutes, and Jake could tell she was thinking about it. He wouldn't leave her out here alone, so if she wasn't ready to move to the bedroom, he'd just stay out here with her. He might have to start looking for a chiropractor, though. He laughed a little bit and rubbed his eyes. He did feel so tired.

JUST HOLD ON

He waited for her answer however it might come.

Slowly, her hand snaked across the blanket, she laced her fingers between his and squeezed his hand.

He'd come to take this as an affirmative answer—*oh, thank God*! He was *so* excited to lay flat tonight. Jake leaned his head back and smiled.

Jake stood and went to the bedroom to fold down the blankets, and as he walked in, he saw the box of pictures. He thought for a moment, and wondered if she never came in here because the pictures were here. Maybe, he should move them. He opened the closet door and slid the box inside. Out of sight, out of mind, he hoped. He left the bedroom door open for a little while, so it could get warmed up.

Jake let the dog out, then helped Marnie down the hall to the bedroom. Barbossa followed. Jake thought it might be a little bit ridiculous, being this excited about sleeping in a bed.

Marnie stood in the doorway briefly, scanning the room with her eyes. Her gaze landed in the place where the box of pictures had been, then she looked back at Jake. He told her what he had done, and she seemed okay with it.

Jake had a thought—what if he could make her laugh? He scooped her up into his arms and said, "Here we go, sweetheart, I'm going to carry you over the threshold." He looked her in the eyes, and even though she didn't laugh out loud he thought he saw a little glimmer that told him she understood the joke. He knew she was in there somewhere.

Marnie laid her head on his shoulder, and let him carry her to the bed.

Barbossa couldn't make the leap up onto the bed. With his missing back leg, he didn't quite have the power to jump that high, so Jake lifted him up. Jake smiled as he watched the dog walk all around the mattress, as if looking for the very best spot to lie down in.

Marnie still lay in the center of the bed, right where he'd put her.

Jake went around the other side of the bed and lifting the covers, slid in behind her. Oh, that felt good, lying flat on his back. After a few minutes though, he realized with so much more room they weren't as close as they'd been on the couch. He kind of missed it. He reached his arm beneath her head, and with his hand on her shoulder pulled her toward him. She curled up like a little child to him, with her head nestled on his shoulder, her face on his chest. The dog settled down and snuggled right up to her back.

Jake could feel Marnie's restlessness. Maybe, he shouldn't have pushed her to move into the bedroom—maybe she wasn't ready for the change. He felt her tossing in the bed, whimpering. Twisting the blankets. She'd been like this for nearly an hour.

He'd been trying to comfort her, get her to settle back down and go back to sleep, but she didn't seem able to. He didn't know what to do for her. "Marnie, honey, if there is anything I can do for you, to help you tonight, just tell me. Look at me, talk to me, show me what you need. I'll do anything for you. It hurts me to see you so miserable."

She turned to him, looking frustrated.

Jake could tell she wanted to communicate with him, but for whatever reason she absolutely could not talk.

He got an idea. "Marnie, if I give you that notebook and a pen, could you write what you need?" If he hadn't been staring at her so intently, he would have missed the slight nod of her head.

Yes! Jake scrambled up and out to the living room—where had he put it? He'd bought that notebook weeks ago and put it—somewhere? *There it is!*

He hurried back to the bedroom, onto the bed. "Here, here you go." Jake felt so excited. What would she say? What would she tell him? He had to admit he did feel a little disappointed when she finished writing so quickly. What was that…oh, she'd only written one word. He turned the notebook toward him so he could read it. She'd written the word: 'Sing'.

Sing? What? "What do you want, Marnie? Do you want—you want me to sing to you? What do you want me to sing?"

One shoulder moved up and down in a little shrug.

He sang often enough, usually when he was cooking or cleaning, but it was just something he'd

JUST HOLD ON

always done. He'd never really sung for anyone else, but he promised her he would do anything she asked, so he thought a moment, trying to think of a song that would settle her spirit. Pulling her toward him, so that her back was against his chest and his arms around her, he sang.

"*Good morning beautiful, how was your night? Mine was wonderful, with you by my side. And when I open my eyes and see your sweet face, it's a good morning beautiful day.....*"

Jake knew all the words to that song. He just loved the lyrics, so he sang it over and over and over. Finally, he felt her start to relax against him. Soon, he could feel her breathing even out. She was asleep.

CHAPTER NINE

*M*orning light shined in through the bedroom window. Jake rubbed his eyes as he woke and glanced over at Marnie. His breath caught in his chest—*Uh-Oh*. Her hair had come out of the braid during the night, probably a result of her tossing and turning. He'd become so accustomed to seeing it either wet or in the long braid and now, for the first time, he was seeing her thick, deep red tresses spread across the pillows, surrounding her like a—like a….

As corny as it sounded in his mind, he could think of no other comparison but to think it looked like a glorious red halo. Or maybe like liquid copper. The color of her hair made such a stark contrast on the white sheets, and the way the light was hitting it, it seemed to sparkle in some places like gold.

Hesitantly, Jake reached out to touch it. He felt a jolt shoot through his body and was struck again, by how incredibly beautiful Marnie was. He couldn't remember ever meeting another woman with such extraordinary looks.

Jake had to stop thinking like this. Yes Marnie was very pretty, but they were friends, drawn together by shared tragedy. She wasn't even well enough to speak, let alone engage in a relationship and furthermore, he was basically her caregiver, not her lover. She trusted him, she depended on him, and he never wanted to hurt her. He never wanted to break her trust in him, or make her disappointed in him.

Okay! Jake clapped his hands and rubbed them together for a moment. *Well, good then. Time to start the day.* He should've made breakfast for Marnie an hour ago, but he knew she hadn't gotten much sleep last night and he wanted to let her rest. He realized this was the first morning since they'd been together that she hadn't woken up in a panic, clutching at him when he started to move. *That had to be a good sign, right?*

It'd only taken two months.

~***~

Jake was dancing around the kitchen, singing for all he was worth. Marnie was sleeping as he made breakfast. His back didn't hurt, the sun was shining and it was a really nice morning. It wouldn't be long, he was thinking, until spring came. Six or seven more weeks until the snow would start to thaw…something else to look forward to.

He bet he could get Marnie outside, once the weather got warmer. Once summer was finally here, and it was warm all the time, they could go to the park. He still hadn't succeeded in getting her out of the house, and knew he would be grateful for the warmer weather.

He suddenly wondered if his leg would still bother him in summer, the way it did now when it

JUST HOLD ON

was cold. Sometimes, the aching kept him awake at night, but this morning his leg didn't hurt. He felt better than he had in a really, really long time. He felt…awake…alive.

He heard a shuffling sound in the kitchen doorway. "Yes, Barbossa, I know. Breakfast is late this morning. I'm getting it. I'm getting it." Jake turned from the counter where he'd been filling the dog's water dish.

Marnie stood in the doorway, leaning against the frame.

Jake was so startled he dropped the dog dish, and it clattered to the floor and smashed. "Marnie? Are you okay? Look at you!" He rushed to her and threw his arms around her. *She was up on her own! Up, dressed, standing up, walking on her own. This was fantastic!* His heart felt as if it were singing for joy. He couldn't remember ever being so happy in his life.

Why is her hair so wet? Jake pulled back and realized he'd been crying—crying into her hair. He touched her face, smiling. She wasn't completely healed yet, but this was certainly a step in the right direction, and he would take what he could get.

Her eyes met his, and he was struck again by what a pretty color green they were—and it seemed like, this morning, there was a little sparkle in them too. A little life. She was waking up, he felt sure of it.

It was a very good morning. Yes, it really was.

And so it went for another few weeks. Marnie still wasn't talking, but Jake had become accustomed to that. Some days were still very, very bad, but other days it seemed like she was beginning to come out of the fog that had engulfed her these last few months. Those were the days Jake started to look for. As happy as he was to see her progress, he did worry sometimes that, once she was fully aware, the reality of all she'd lost would hit her hard.

Jake noticed the more days she was able to get herself up, dressed and then walk to the living room on her own, the more nights she seemed to have restless sleep and nightmares.

Occasionally, the nightmares would wake her up, and he would hold her and sing until she fell

JUST HOLD ON

back to sleep. He didn't mind...if he could just help her get through this part, this darkest time, someday they would get through to the other side and she would be better. They both would be.

After a couple of weeks though, the nightmares seemed to be getting worse. Some nights, Marnie would thrash about so much that neither of them was able to get any sleep. On those nights, Jake would lay there in the darkness, feeling helpless. One particularly bad night, Marnie had been crying out in her sleep. As much as he longed to hear her voice, Jake hated hearing it this way—so broken, so pitiful. He almost preferred the silence.

Jake kept trying to think of some way to engage Marnie. Some way to communicate with her. He thought it may help quicken her recovery if he could get her mind focused on something and he wondered if she liked to play games—or if she would even be able to in her current mental state.

While out running errands one day, he stopped at Wal-Mart and bought two games: *Aggravation* and *Scrabble*. He brought them home and set them on the table, then went into the kitchen to start dinner. He was making homemade pizza tonight, always trying to focus on making food for Marnie that would help strengthen her to help her gain weight.

When he carried her plate to the living room, he was pleased to see she was already sitting up on the couch. Dragging a kitchen chair so that he was sitting directly in front of her, he cut the pizza into small pieces to feed her.

Jake felt truly startled when Marnie reached her hand out, unsteadily at first and took the fork from his hand. He released it and watched with pride as she fed herself for the first time in more than three months. He wondered if this was how a parent felt when their child first learned to walk and he wished so badly that he had someone he could call. Someone else to share his joy. Instead, he looked away and blinked as he felt his eyes well up.

Again. Good grief, he was getting soppy in his dotage. Could you even be in dotage before forty? Apparently. Cognitive decline was likely just around the corner for him. He felt far, far older than his years. Wait a minute—it was the end of March. His

JUST HOLD ON

birthday was April 2. Hard to believe he was only turning 36. He'd been spending his birthdays alone for ten years now.

Occasionally, he thought this was a time when it might be nice to have a couple of friends, but he never really did anything special since there was never anybody to do it with.

This year, though, was different. He did have someone. His relationship with Marnie, he knew, wasn't typical. Some people may not even agree that it was a relationship, but it was—Jake knew this with certainty. She trusted him, and he trusted her. He told her things he hadn't shared with anyone else…ever. Maybe it's because she never talked to him about it after he told her, but he liked to think it was because he was comfortable with her.

True, she depended on him for most things, but he depended on her too. Maybe not for basic survival, but he depended on Marnie for other things, and he thought they were just as important. Being with Marnie had helped him open up places in his soul he thought he'd shut off forever. While that was painful at times, it'd also been good for him. He could see now how sad and lonely his life had been before.

Jake knew she cared about him, because on bad days, when he broke down and cried, or his leg bothered him a great deal, she would turn and hold him, resting her hand on his head and her cheek on his hair.

Jake was realizing that his long ago decision not to care about anybody else may not have been the best choice. While it certainly saved him the grief of loving and losing, it also robbed him of the joys of loving someone and the peace of knowing someone else cared for him. And Jake knew now, that he did love Marnie. No, he wasn't *in love* with her, but he did love her.

He really didn't believe in falling in love. Love wasn't some hole in the ground you tripped and fell into; it was a conscious choice. Either you chose to love somebody, or you chose not to. He'd decided to stop loving his father and he'd chosen to love Alexis, and then he chose to stop. Now, after ten years, he was choosing to love again.

JUST HOLD ON

He was investing in Marnie's life and their souls were so entangled he couldn't imagine separating them. Every day, all day, they were together and by the very nature of their relationship, they did come to know each other in an incredibly intimate way.

Even without an ability to speak, he felt he knew Marnie better than he'd ever known another person. They had no secrets. He'd known her during the very worst time of her life—when grief just swallowed her up so completely, she was just a shell of herself—and still he cared for her. He'd fed her, and carried her when she couldn't walk. He'd bathed her, although he hadn't attempted any more bubble baths, dressed her and brushed her hair.

He learned through her photo albums of the love and loss she endured, and that drew them closer together. He knew she'd been a devoted wife and loving mother. He knew she was brave, because she kept her life going after losing her husband, trying to make a future for her little girl.

Jake really couldn't imagine what else there would be to know about a person.

And Marnie knew him. During the hours and days that Marnie wasn't able to function at all, and he'd spent most of every day holding her on the couch, he talked to her about his life. He even told her about his childhood, and how he always wanted to become a teacher. Of how happy he'd been when his parents announced he would have a new little sister—although most boys his age would have been upset, he'd been thrilled.

Jake shared with her about how, when he went off to college, he would come home most weekends, so he could take Cassie and her friends out to the movies, or bowling, or to the mall. He even told Marnie how his father left his mother eleven years ago and they hadn't heard from him since, and the effect it had on his mother.

But he *hadn't* told her Cassie died, or how it happened. Jake did explain to Marnie about Alexis, and his decision to break things off with her. How he decided to live his life alone, without the complications of relationships and the emotional toll they always brought with them.

JUST HOLD ON

One night, after he spent an hour reading to her...as had become their evening routine. He explained to her how much he appreciated the relationship they shared, and that it meant so much to him how she trusted him enough to allow him to care for her.

Of course, she never said anything back, but she did take his hand and squeeze it.

He knew what she meant.

CHAPTER TEN

"Marnie? Guess what! Today, we're going to do something different. Know why? Because today is my birthday, and I haven't spent my birthday with anyone in a decade. You're the special girl, breaking that lonely drought. I'm going to buy a cake and we're going to eat it together. And then, because it's my birthday and you are obligated to give me a gift, I'm going to tell you what I want my gift to be. Well, as I've said before, what I would like most from you is to hear your voice. But—you know, no pressure…"

He waited a few seconds and watched her absorb what he said.

"After that, what I would like most is for you to spend the evening playing some games with me. A

JUST HOLD ON

few weeks ago, I bought Aggravation and Scrabble, and I want you to come over here, to the dining table to eat cake and play these games with me. It's my birthday, and I get to choose what we do today. Now, when it's your birthday, whenever that is...I guess I don't even know—then you get to pick what we do that day. And I'll do it. Whatever you ask me to do, I promise. And you know, I always keep the promises I make to you."

Marnie tilted her head, as she seemed to listen to him.

"So, come on. I'm going to go to the bakery and pick up my cake, and when I get back we'll cut it and eat the whole thing together while we play. I want you ready when I get back."

Jake whistled as he walked through the grocery store to the bakery section and picked out a cake. He decided to get the most ridiculous cake he could, so he picked up a very pink cake: strawberry flavored, light pink frosting, dark pink piping across the top that said ,"Happy Birthday!"

He asked the baker to add "Baby-cakes" to the top. Then, he bought some tiny plastic balloons to stick on top and just for a little something extra, a small plastic Tweety Bird that held a tiny sign saying, "Happy Birthday, Puddytat." He dared Marnie not to laugh at this…he just dared her.

"Honey, I'm home!" he joked as he carried his birthday bounty through the door. Jake smiled so wide he thought his face might crack at the sight of Marnie sitting up at the dining table, with Barbossa on the chair next to her. She'd even taken out the Aggravation game and set it up for them.

He blinked rapidly as he took the cake and ice-cream to the kitchen. This was really getting to be a problem—maybe he should see a doctor about it. Maybe he had some kind of…leaky eye disorder or something, and could take a pill to make it stop. It was getting to be a bit ridiculous, this eye leaking thing.

"Happy birthday to me, happy birthday to me," Jake sang as he carried his cake, complete with lit candles, to the table. He sat it down, and waited for some reaction.

Marnie stared at it, looked up at Jake, and raised an eyebrow. Then the most amazing thing

JUST HOLD ON

happened: she smiled. Well, not a full-on toothy smile, but the left side of her mouth raised in a smirk as she stared at the ridiculous looking cake, then up at Jake.

He felt like he'd won the lottery. No, better than the lottery. There was no amount of money worth more to him than her smile. Well—smirk actually.

Jake blew out the candles and cut the cake, scooping some ice cream on the plates and handing Marnie a fork.

She took a few bites—he was still so tickled about it every time he watched her eat on her own—and then reached down under her chair and brought up a folded piece of paper, which she handed to him.

Curious, he took it and read it. *Damn it, his freaking eyes!* He wiped at his blurry vision and took a deep breath.

It was a homemade birthday card, which read, "Jake. Thank you. Happy Birthday. How old?"

Jake was just undone. He quit messing with his eyes, because there was no point, he couldn't make the tears stop. He let his head fall into his hands, elbows on the table. Quietly, he wept.

Marnie patted his head and stroked his hair until he stopped.

"Thank you, Marnie, thank you. This means so much to me. This is the greatest gift I've ever been given. Do you know that? Do you know how much you mean to me? You mean so much. I—I care about you so much, Marnie. You're—you're my best friend. You really are. I'm so thankful, Marnie, that I'm lucky enough to spend this day with you. Okay, okay, are you ready for our fun night? Let's get our game started, I'm really looking forward to this."

Not so fast. Marnie grabbed his wrist, looked him in the eye, her gaze darting back to the open card on the table.

"What?"

Marnie tapped her foot, motioning her head back at the card.

Jake followed her line of vision. "Oh. You want to know how old I am today? Old. Very old. Decrepit, even. I'm 36, Marnie. Ancient. Ha! I'm old enough to be your—uh—well, I'm old enough to be your older brother!" While he said it, he realized if Marnie was about 23, as he guessed, it would've been the age Cassie would be, if she had lived. His chest hurt for a minute.

He'd never thought of Cassie as an adult—would she have gotten married? Had a child by now? In his mind, she always remained the child she'd been when she died. Cassie was forever 13.

Enough of this—this was going to be a happy day.

That night, as they lay together on the couch watching *Law & Order*, Jake twirled a long strand of Marnie's hair around his finger. "Thank you, Marnie. Today was the best birthday I've had since—since I can't even remember. It was fun playing games with you…maybe we could do that again sometime. Would you like that?" He brushed some hair away from her face and kissed the top of her hair. "Thank you, Marnie. Thank you." He drifted off to sleep that way.

VALARIE SAVAGE KINNEY

~***~

Marnie watched Jake sleep. She did this often, but she didn't think he knew. She was beginning to feel better, stronger. Sometimes, she felt as if she'd gotten a new pair of glasses, the world was beginning to look so different to her. Everything seemed to be getting brighter, sharper, more focused.

When she watched TV now, she understood what was going on. When she listened to Jake reading to her, she could follow the story. She loved it when he read to her, and when he sang—he had such a strong, deep voice. He'd been so patient with her these last several months.

At first, after the fire, she felt so empty, so lost. Sometimes, she would wake up and not be able to remember if it was the same day, or the next one. She had no sense of time at all. She often felt like she was stuck in some strange fog, where she couldn't see or think straight, and didn't know what direction to move in. If she'd been left alone, she felt sure she would have died. She felt very grateful to this kind man—Jake.

He was an unusual man. She didn't think she'd ever known another man who would have done this—who would have given up his life to move in with her and care for her when she wasn't capable of caring for herself.

Marnie thought of the day of Katie's funeral—the hardest day of her life. She'd felt so alone, and remembered thinking that if only Daniel had been there with her, she could have gotten through it. But Daniel was gone, too. She was alone. Her father died when she was a little girl, and she had no siblings. Her mother died a few years ago, from a rare and aggressive form of lung cancer. When her mother died, it'd been terribly hard, but she'd had Daniel to cling to, and he'd been so supportive. When Daniel died, she thought she couldn't go on, but she'd had Katie to think of. She knew she needed to be strong for Katie, just the way her own mother had been.

Marnie redirected her grief into loving her little girl, but when Katie died...she'd had no one. She

just wanted to die. There was no point in living;
she'd had no one left to live for.

She remembered now, sitting there in that awful
room, alone on the couch, waiting for the funeral
service for her baby to begin, wishing she could die
before it started. She hadn't wanted to be there,
listening to the pastor drone on about Katie being in
a better place, or watching her precious daughter
being lowered into the ground in the little white box.

Then Jake came in and sat with her. She
couldn't show him how much it meant to her at the
time, she wasn't able to give anything to anyone.
But she remembered his strong arms around her
when she collapsed, and how tightly he'd held her
when she was shaking so hard. He was her only
anchor, the only person in the world who cared
about her. She didn't know why he did, but she felt
grateful for it.

The night of the fire was still a blur to her, but
she could recall some things. She remembered the
absolute horror of finding Katie trapped in her crib,
smoke filling the apartment. She tried so hard to free
her baby, and hadn't even realized she'd been

JUST HOLD ON

screaming for help until Jake arrived. Marnie hadn't known him well, but she'd recognized him from the day he helped her with the groceries. That day, she did think it was a kind thing for him to do. The sort of thing Daniel would have done for somebody.

The night of the fire, she hadn't even heard him bust the door in. Suddenly, he just appeared there, looking so ridiculous. Wearing only jeans and a winter hat with furry flaps pulled down over his head, barefoot and with no shirt, holding the little black dog. If it hadn't been such a horrifying situation, he would have looked hilarious.

He himself tried so hard, she knew that. She didn't blame him for Katie's death. Jake stayed inside with the fire blazing, risking his life to get Katie out of the crib. She could picture him carrying Katie out through the smashed window, and running with her to get her safely away from the fire.

Clearly, she could see him repeating CPR, over and over. She thought he must have done it dozens of times. There he'd been, the gash in his leg bleeding uncontrollably, his jeans torn. He couldn't breathe well himself, but he'd been giving all his breath for her little girl.

No, Katie's death wasn't his fault, but she wondered sometimes, if he blamed himself. One day, she was going to tell him that it wasn't his fault. One day, she was going to tell him a lot of things.

Watching him sleeping, she had to admit he was a very attractive man. Black hair with just a hint of gray starting to creep in, and it was usually worn kind of long and shaggy looking. She wondered if it was the look he actually wanted, or if he just had trouble remembering to go get it cut regularly, with no one to remind him to do it.

Marnie noticed how the longer his hair grew, the curlier it became. Sometimes, he would go a week or more without shaving his face. Like right now, he had a good amount of dark stubble covering his jawline. He'd fallen asleep with his glasses on and a book in his hand…again.

Funny, how he bathed her and brushed her hair out meticulously, but was so careless with his own looks.

Her gaze drifted down to his hands.

JUST HOLD ON

Such strong hands. Beautiful hands.

Those hands held her through the worst grief of her life, held her tightly through her bad days and when she woke up with nightmares. Those hands bathed her tenderly and brushed the tangles from her long hair, day after day. Those hands fed her and made her drink when she was unable to do it for herself. Those same hands had broken through the crib that held her daughter captive; they carried Katie out of the burning building; they performed CPR over and over, even when there was no hope for revival.

Marnie curled up beside him, lacing her fingers through his. Jake did have such beautiful hands.

She wished she could communicate with him. She knew he wanted her to speak to him, but she just—couldn't. Marnie knew, without a doubt, that if she started to talk, everything she'd been holding inside of her these last months would burst forth, like water rushing through a broken dam, and she would start to cry and never be able to stop.

She knew wasn't ready for that just yet. The nightmares were enough of an emotional toll. She wasn't sure what was better—being dead and empty inside with no emotions, the way she had been for such a long time, or feeling like—well, *feeling*. This was what was happening now. She was starting to feel everything again.

Marnie felt the keen loss of her husband, and the pitiful loss of her little girl. The lost future they would never have together. She felt the loss of her home and the new life she hoped to begin here. Some days, it hurt so much, she wished she could go back to being a zombie again, but sometimes, the feelings were good too.

The warmth of the sun shining through the window and the strength in Jake's arms when he held her. The little spark of joy when Barbossa insisted on only sitting near her, when he would curl up and stay with her for hours. She was even beginning to taste food again, and someday, she really needed to tell Jake she didn't enjoy chocolate milkshakes. But even that, tasting something she didn't really like, became a good feeling, because at least, she *could* taste it now.

JUST HOLD ON

Marnie felt sorry for Jake. He seemed just as alone as she was. She knew his mother must still be alive, because occasionally, he would say he was going to visit her, but he didn't seem especially close to her. She wondered what caused Jake's father to walk out on his family, but Jake never told her. Marnie wondered why Jake never spoke about Cassie in the present tense. She knew he loved her fiercely, but he never told her a story about Cassie where she was older than 12 or 13.

Something must have happened to the girl—maybe she had run away? *Cassie had obviously done something to hurt Jake so intensely.* Marnie knew there was something Jake wasn't being totally honest about, and one day, she intended to ask Jake about Cassie.

It seemed to her at about the same time his dad left, and the same time Jake left his teaching job, was right around the time, the Cassie stories ended.

CHAPTER ELEVEN

Marnie was having another nightmare. Jake already tried waking her, but it didn't seem like she could hear him. He'd been holding her for close to an hour, helplessly watching as she grew more and more agitated. She kept whimpering like a wounded animal, reaching her arms out to grasp something he couldn't see.

Was it Katie? Daniel? Jake wished he could give her whatever it was she seemed so desperate to reach. *Uh-oh.* He could feel her stomach beginning to lurch—that couldn't be good. He leapt from the bed to get the small trash can he kept in the bedroom, just in time for her to wake from the nightmare and start to vomit. He patted her back and

JUST HOLD ON

held her braid until it was over, and she fell back onto the bed, completely spent.

Silently, Jake cleaned the mess and brought Marnie a washcloth to wipe her face. This was becoming a regular occurrence, and Jake had no idea what to do about it. The more alert Marnie appeared throughout the day, the worse she seemed at night. During the day, she was up more, showering on her own, feeding herself, flipping the channels on the TV. Then, at night, she grew restless, twisting herself up in the blankets, crying out and breaking into a sweat. Often, it all culminated in an episode of vomiting. It almost seemed to him, that her body was trying to purge itself of something toxic.

Tonight, as he did most nights now, he held her and sang until she fell asleep.

"*I set out on a narrow way, many years ago.*

Hoping I would find true love, along the broken road.

But I got lost a time or two.

Wiped my brow, kept pushing through.

I couldn't see how every sign...Pointed straight to you...."

"Marnie," he whispered into the darkness, "I'm so grateful for you. I know I've said this before, but I really mean it. You're my best friend, the best friend I've ever had. I didn't realize how lonely I'd been until you came into my life, and I'm so thankful that you've helped me realize I needed a friend. I needed someone in my life. You mean so much to me."

They both fell asleep just as the sun was beginning to stream through the windows. It'd been a long night.

The next day, Jake noticed something unexpected and new.

Marnie seemed to be writing in her notebook. At first, Jake thought she was writing something to him, but now he wasn't so sure.

She'd been writing for close to an hour, and since she wasn't sharing it with him, it must be something private. *That is good, maybe she was writing her feelings out. At least, she's getting them out somehow.* He went about the evening's domestic duties: cooking dinner, cleaning up after and settling down to get started on a work assignment. He

JUST HOLD ON

glanced up at Marnie, and she was still scribbling away in the notebook. At least, she'd become cognizant enough to be able to do that.

~***~

The following morning brought a beautiful sunshiny day. Barbossa kept climbing up on the edge of the couch, so he could look out the window.

After breakfast, Jake went to take a shower and Marnie got herself dressed. She felt really good today. Strong. She'd been thinking of doing this for a while, but kept talking herself out of it. Today was going to be the big day, though. She knew Jake didn't have work to do today, because he mentioned last night how he was finished for the week.

After she finished dressing, she went to the closet and took out the coat Jake bought for her. He'd brought it home several weeks ago in the hopes he could get her to go somewhere with him, but she hadn't been ready then. Today, she was. She pulled the tags off the coat and slipped it on, then went to sit on the couch to wait for Jake and surprise him.

She knew this would make him happy, and she liked making him happy.

Jake did have a fantastic smile, and whenever she did something new to show she was getting better, his smile would just light up his face, eyes sparkling. It made her feel warm inside when she could do that for him.

The water from his shower stopped…she'd been listening. Marnie could hear Jake singing in the bathroom as he dressed. He walked out, rubbing at his hair with a towel.

She smiled to herself, because again, his hair was really getting long, and when it was wet, it curled up into perfect little coils.

~***~

Jake stopped dead in his tracks when he saw her, standing near the couch in her new coat. His eyes met hers, and held for a few seconds. "The coat looks good on you, Marnie. Does it fit?" he asked, cautiously. He didn't want to get his hopes up—he wasn't sure what this meant. *Was she just trying it on?*

Marnie nodded, then held her hand out and slowly opened up her fist. She was holding his car keys!

"Marnie—do you want to go someplace? Are you ready to go outside?"

Briefly, she nodded again.

"Okay! Okay, this is great! Okay—you stay here, I'll be right back. I'll go fast, just let me—get my…Please don't change your mind, I'll be ready in just a second."

Jake was lacing his shoes up, grinning, hands trembling. He was beyond excited. When he looked up, he saw Marnie holding Barbossa's leash, hooking it onto his collar. *Of course, she wouldn't want to leave without him…*He'd been her constant companion for more than four months now.

Slowly, the trio made their way down the hall and to the door.

Marnie slowed down and then paused.

Jake looked down at her. "You can do this. I know you can." He placed his hand against the small of her back and gently guided her out into the parking lot.

Marnie stopped for a moment, blinking in the bright sunlight, as if it hurt her eyes. She took a deep breath, grasped Jake's hand in hers, and they walked out to his car.

Jake opened the door for her and helped settle her in, then brought Barbossa up onto her lap. He didn't want to pressure her too much, and he didn't think she would be ready to be out in a crowd yet. He asked where she wanted to go, and she just shrugged her shoulders. He then, thought it might be nice to drive out through some of the country, maybe even over to the waterfront. It was early enough in the day, they could drive for a few hours. They really had nothing to hurry for.

He glanced over at her and saw she was holding onto Barbossa tightly. *This is really a big step for her.*

They set off, driving through town, then out to some back roads where it became more country looking and the houses were spaced farther apart. Lots of old farmhouses out this way.

JUST HOLD ON

Jake always thought this was a pretty area. The sky appeared to be such a vibrant blue, the clouds so perfectly fluffy hanging in the sky. It seemed to Jake the day must have been made just for Marnie. He turned up the radio a little, and started singing along.

They drove for over an hour until they came to the waterfront area, and he parked near the dock that led to the lighthouse, quite a ways away from the little cluster of people down on the beach. They sat in the car for a bit, then Jake got out and opened the trunk.

Marnie watched while looking curious.

Jake always kept a heavy blanket in the trunk, in case he had car trouble in the winter. Carrying it, he walked just a few feet from the side of the car and laid the blanket out flat, smoothing the wrinkles away with his hand.

~***~

Marnie watched him through the window, knowing in her heart what he intended to do and she felt frightened. Of what, she didn't know—she just felt afraid. She looked around again, and there was no one anywhere near them.

Jake opened the door, took the dog out and set him down, then reached under Marnie's knees with one arm, then around her neck with the other and carried her to the blanket.

She kept shivering, though it wasn't very cold out and she had her coat on.

Jake sat down behind her, stretching his legs around her small frame, folding her into his warm embrace and settling his chin on her shoulder.

Barbossa circled them, sniffing several spots before deciding, as he usually did, to curl up near Marnie.

The pair watched the waves crashing against the rocks, surrounding the lighthouse. It felt good to both of them to be outside, the sun beaming down on them, the wind blowing just a little bit. They stayed that way for a long time, until they were both probably a little chilled.

Without a word, Jake helped Marnie back to the car, loaded the dog in, folded up the blanket and returned it to the trunk.

JUST HOLD ON

Then they set off for home.

~*** ~

    This had been a great idea. Marnie's cheeks were flushed with color, her green eyes bright and shining. They should do this more often, Jake thought. Maybe next time, he could bring a lunch for them to eat.

    Back home, Jake set about cooking their evening meal, and Marnie went back to scribbling in her notebook. He felt very curious about what she was writing and tempted to sneak a peek, but he wouldn't do that to her. He never wanted to do anything that would break the trust she put in him. He thought about just asking her what was in it—not that it was really his business.

    While they sat together at the table eating dinner, his gaze kept traveling over to the notebook.

    Marnie watched him for a bit, then stood up, grabbed the notebook and brought it back to him.

    Jake felt shocked—just shocked. All this time, he thought she'd been writing in the tablet, but as he flipped through the pages, he saw she hadn't been writing at all. She'd been drawing, and she was an incredible artist. Jake marveled at her talent. He felt as if he were watching the last few years of her life emerge from those pages.

The first page was Daniel, whom he recognized from the photo albums. Daniel knelt down on one knee, holding up an engagement ring, a nervous but happy expression on his face. The next page, Marnie's hand—Jake would know her hand anywhere—with the ring on, fingers laced together with what must be Daniel's hand, his ring finger sporting a wedding band.

Another picture, this one of Marnie, her belly slightly swollen, her hands holding her dress close to her body to show off the life growing within her.

Jake's damn eyes were leaking again. These were her most precious memories, he was certain. The pages were filled with drawings like these.

The next drawing was of Daniel, his shirt off, holding a tiny Katie curled against his chest, both of them sleeping. Jake wasn't sure he could take looking at any more, but he knew it must be hard for

JUST HOLD ON

Marnie to share her memories. This was one way she could communicate with him, so he forced himself to keep turning the pages.

The last few years of her life were playing out before his eyes and when he got to the end, he realized she had used up all the pages. "Marnie, do you need another notebook? Or, would you rather have a sketch pad, with larger paper?"

She nodded.

"Okay, I'll go out tomorrow and buy you some more. As many as you want." Jake made a mental note to buy not only sketchpads, but more pencils, colored pencils, charcoal—anything she could use to draw with. He tried to remember what kinds of the things the art teacher at the school he used to teach at used in her class.

After he brought it all home, Marnie drew and drew.

Jake wondered that her hands didn't cramp from so much drawing. At times, she looked almost feverish in her mission to get a picture just right. He never looked at her drawings, unless she offered to let him see them. It seemed like they were always of the three of them, either alone or together: Daniel, Marnie, Katie. Lots of pictures of Daniel in his military uniform. Then, even more of Katie as she grew.

Jake kept Marnie supplied with sketch pads, sometimes going back out a few times a week to buy her more pencils and pads, because he thought the drawing was good for her. To him, it seemed like the more she drew, the better she slept.

She finally seemed to be having fewer nightmares and even when she did, he thought they must not be quite as awful as before, because she rarely threw up now.

Sometimes though, he would feel her slip out of bed during the night, and when he went to check on her, she would be out in the living room, drawing.

He let her be. She seemed really to need this time and Jake could see she was working through something.

CHAPTER TWELVE

*I*t was a Tuesday morning. Summer was in full swing now and weather permitting, Jake would take Marnie and Barbossa to the waterfront a couple of times a week. He'd taken to packing a picnic lunch for them on the days they went, and always—always he packed Marnie's sketch pad and pencils.

They would park as far down from the crowds as they could, and so far no one had wandered over to their secluded spot. Sometimes, Jake would bring a work project to fiddle with. Marnie would lie on the blanket and draw, and they would often spend an entire day there.

Barbossa loved these outings, he would sprint around in the sand, occasionally running down to the water and splashing in the shallows until he wore himself out.

Today, as they sat together on their blanket, Jake pulled out a calendar to review which work assignments he had due this week and the date struck him like a blow. Today was the sixth of July. The fire had been on the sixth day of January. *Six months, exactly.* He considered how much both of their lives had changed in six months.

Marnie reached back, touching his arm to get his attention.

Putting aside his work, he scooted closer to her on the blanket.

She handed him the sketch pad she'd been drawing in for the last two hours.

Jake stared down at the page, expecting to see another drawing of Daniel. What the…?

Jake was looking at himself. Eyebrows furrowed, he sat back to study the picture. It felt strange, seeing his face come to life on a piece of paper like this, and she certainly captured the details of his features, his expression.

Here, he looked like he was walking away from a fire, flames blazing in the distance behind him, clad only in jeans, feet bare. He hadn't had time to

JUST HOLD ON

grab a shirt *that* night, he remembered, or shoes. *Why was he wearing that hat?* He laughed—he remembered now. He grabbed it on the way out. The furry flaps hung down over his ears, and in the crook of his left arm sat Barbossa, staring straight out.

He felt struck again by her incredible talent, but thought Marnie may have been a bit generous when drawing the way his muscles looked. Hey, that was okay with him. Jake leaned over and gave her a little hug, kissing the top of her head. "Hey, I look pretty hot in this picture, don't I? And not just because of the flames," he joked.

Marnie smiled up at him, took back her tablet, and went right back to drawing.

~***~

When Marnie first handed the notebook to Jake, she knew she needed to finally share it with him; to show him what she'd been doing over the last weeks. She knew he was curious, plus she filled her notebook and wanted another one.

Marnie watched as he opened the first page, then slowly flipped through the rest. Different emotions played across his face: confusion, joy, sadness.

Marnie now watched Jake getting ready for the day. He walked around in jeans and a white shirt unbuttoned. He never used to do that, but she supposed that he'd become more comfortable with her lately. His hair still looked wet from a shower, and he had those little springy coils bouncing around again. He was singing as he made a pot of coffee.

She wondered where he might be going today. She noticed he sometimes went out for a few hours, but didn't come back with anything from a store. Marnie didn't know where he went on those days. Hastily, she tore a corner from her sketch book and wrote… *"Where are you going?"* Then, handed it to him.

Jake read the note and gazed up at her, looking surprised. "Um, actually, I'm going to visit my mom. Like I said before, she lives in a home for

JUST HOLD ON

people with problems like she has. I try to get over there to see her at least a few times a month. I don't know if she really even understands that I'm there, but it makes me feel bad not to visit her."

Marnie stared at him.

"Would you like to come with me? I'd really enjoy it if you did. I'm the only one who ever visits her, and I know she would probably like to see a new face. She doesn't say much, but then again, neither do you, I guess."

She swallowed heavily, thinking about what a sweet man he always is. Caring for people who couldn't even speak—like her.

"Please, Marnie? You don't have to talk, just come in and sit with me. It's a small place; there are only about six residents there. It's not ever crowded or anything. Nobody will bother you. Please? Come with me?"

Marnie considered this for a moment. She wasn't as frightened to leave the apartment as she used to be. Their days at the waterfront really helped to ease that fear. But those days were different. They were out, but she didn't have to deal with anyone else, when they went. Jake has been so good to her, though. He rarely asked her for anything, and this seemed like it meant a lot to him. She would do it. She would force herself to go—for Jake. She would do anything for Jake...

~***~

Jake felt so excited...he really wanted his mom to meet Marnie. As they walked into the large rambling farmhouse, he could feel Marnie trembling. He placed his hand on the small of her back for support, opened the door and waved to the nurse as they walked to his mother's room.

Good grief—another jogging suit! Dark purple this time and his mother looked like a giant grape. Or, a blueberry. "He experienced a sudden vision of an elderly Veruca Salt...the girl-turned-blueberry from Charlie and the Chocolate Factory."

Why did the nurses keep dressing her like this? *And her hair!* What have they done to his mother's hair? It was one of those—what did women call them? The thing that made their hair all curly?

JUST HOLD ON

Perm—that's what they were called. Someone had put a perm in his mother's hair, and it looked awful.

Jake felt a wave of sadness. A distinct loss for the woman he'd known, the mother he had grown up with. He thought back to his childhood. His mother had been taller than the average woman, with long brown hair, always done up in the latest fashion. She would never have left the house without her earrings on, lipstick and nails painted. His mother had been classy, sharp. Jake remembered how proud he felt when his mom had come up to his school for some reason or other and he would hear people—sometimes even boys his age—comment on her beauty.

It was difficult now, to reconcile the woman he remembered with the shrunken shell before him. *Jogging suits and hair perms, for crying out loud.*

"Mom? I brought someone to meet you today. This is my friend, Marnie. She's the best, Mom. Isn't she beautiful?"

Marnie stepped forward and held out her hand. She kept looking at his mother, trying to catch her eye. She knelt down in front of the chair, holding his mother's hands in hers, and smiled.

Jake's mother peered down at Marnie, confused. "Cassie?" she whispered. "Cassie, baby, is that you? Oh, my baby girl!" She threw her arms around Marnie, holding tight.

Marnie looked a little bit alarmed.

"Mom! No, this isn't Cassie, Mom. MOM! Look at me! This is Marnie, my friend. Cassie isn't here anymore. Remember?" Jake attempted to pry his mother's arms away from Marnie. Boy, for an older woman she had quite a grip.

"Cassie isn't here? Where is she then? Where did my baby go?" Bewildered, his mother began to cry.

Oh boy, Jake thought, this wasn't a good idea after all. He didn't know what to do, so he went out and got the nurse. He came back, dropped a kiss on his mother's head and they left.

Back in the car, he pulled from the drive, trying to think of what to say to Marnie. She seemed kind of shaken up and he really felt bad about it. He hadn't expected his mother to do something like

JUST HOLD ON

that—he'd never seen her do anything like this before. Marnie looked nothing like his sister.

Cassie was tall, where Marnie had a very slight, small frame. Cassie had dark brown hair like their mother's, which she always kept cut a little shorter, because she was into sports and didn't want it to get in her face while she played. Cassie also had brown eyes…they looked nothing alike.

His poor mom. Jake felt bad for her, but had no idea how to make things better for her.

Marnie reached her hand across the front seat and slipped it into his, and he was glad it didn't seem like she felt angry or upset.

Once home, they followed the same little routine they did just about every night, since they started living together.

Jake cooked dinner and set the table, while Marnie rested on the couch. After dinner, Jake sat down on the couch with her, picked up the book they'd been reading and he read to her.

~***~

VALARIE SAVAGE KINNEY

Marnie watched as he brought the book up closer to his face, then back out a little further, squinting just a bit. She thought he may need a different prescription, bifocals or something. She should make him go see the eye doctor, because she didn't think he would go unless someone pushed him to do it.

Marnie tried to focus on the story, on Jake's voice, but her thoughts seemed scattered tonight. She thought of Jake's mother, small and scared in her purple jogging suit. What a sad woman; Marnie felt so sorry for her. She wondered what had happened to make Jake's mother that way.

Jake and Daniel were very different men. Both good men, just different. Daniel had been very gregarious, always surrounded by friends and the first one to show up at any party. Almost every weekend, he would have plans for them to go somewhere.

Left to her own devices, Marnie was more of a homebody. She would rather have a few good friends she could be close with, rather than the flocks of friends Daniel had. She hadn't minded his

JUST HOLD ON

friends, though they were nice enough people and sometimes, it could be fun spending time with them.

Jake certainly wasn't outgoing the way Daniel had been. Marnie knew from the things Jake told her that he had intentionally kept people at a distance for the last ten years. She understood he hadn't wanted anyone to be close to him, and she even understood why he'd been very hurt when his dad left.

But it was more than that. She'd noticed when they were out, if they went through a fast food drive-thru, Jake acted very awkward just putting in an order. He seemed uncomfortable around people, this much was clear. When he spoke to his boss on the phone, he would fidget and shift his weight back and forth in nervousness.

Jake never acted that way with Marnie, though. She'd watched him enough to know whenever he said, 'Okay' and ran his fingers through his hair a lot it meant he felt anxious. Marnie wondered if he'd always been an especially nervous person, or if events in his life made him that way. She knew he didn't have any friends, aside from her.

Marnie pushed her attention back to Jake, trying to catch up with the story he was reading to her, then she got an idea. Abrupt-like, she scribbled a note on a little piece of her paper, tore it off and handed it to him.

He took it and read it.

"Tell me what Cassie looks like."

Jake paused and stared at Marnie for a moment.

I bet he wonders why she wanted to know that. Nonetheless, it was communication, and he always tried to encourage communication of any kind with Marnie. He said he hoped it would lead to a day when she would start talking to him.

"Okay, okay, well—Cassie was tall, like our mom. Taller than most girls her age. She had dark brown hair which she kept all one length, cut right below her chin and it would kind of…kind of curl around her face. Her eyes were brown and shaped like mine."

Marnie watched his eyes lose their focus, taking on a dreamy quality. "She was always into sports, from the time she was little. She was a basketball star in the middle school, just a natural at the game.

JUST HOLD ON

Her arms and legs were long and thin. In the summer, she would get a little sprinkle of freckles across her nose."

It was just as Marnie thought before—Jake was describing a young girl. She moved her fingers into the shape of a rectangle and held them up to her eyes, moving her forefinger in a clicking motion.

Jake looked as if he were trying imagine what she was trying to convey. "What—a camera? Do you want me to buy you a camera?"

Marnie shook her head, pointing to her sketch pad.

"Your pictures? I don't get what you're trying to say, honey."

Marnie leaned forward, taking back the piece of paper she'd written on. She pointed to Cassie's name, then repeated the same motions.

Jake watched and thought for a moment. "A picture of Cassie? Is that what you want?"

Marnie nodded.

"Oh...let me see. I think I have one in my wallet." Jake fumbled through his wallet, wincing a little. He handed it to Marnie

She took it and sat back, studying it. There it was, a picture of Cassie in her basketball uniform, holding a ball and smiling for the camera.

Jake and Cassie did resemble one another. Same eyes, same dark, curly hair, though Cassie's was a little lighter in color.

CHAPTER THIRTEEN

When Jake had reached into his wallet, he realized the pictures he kept there were the only pictures he had left. His boxes of pictures he kept in his closet at the old place had all burned, and the thought hurt his heart a bit.

Marnie flipped her sketchbook open and settled into the corner of the couch, using a paper clip to attach Cassie's picture to her paper.

Jake sighed, he had a good idea of what she was doing. He watched her for a moment, then went back to reading his book.

An hour passed, then Marnie tapped his shoulder, holding her finished drawing up for him to see.

Jake's chest hurt for a minute and tears sprang to his eyes. It was a picture of Cassie and Jake. He was standing with his arm around his sister, her head tilted onto his shoulder. They were both smiling, happy.

Tears started streaming down his face. He traced the outline of Cassie's face with his finger. She'd been so beautiful, his little sister. He missed her so much. He had no pictures of him and Cassie together anymore, and this meant a lot to him. "Thank you, Marnie. This is beautiful, perfect. It looks just like her. Thank you." Jake gulped, trying to stop the sobs from escaping. It was no use, however, because no matter what he did, he couldn't stop crying. He put his head down on the arm of the couch, weeping while remembering the day Cassie died.

Marnie slid closer to him, wrapping her arms around him. For a change, tonight Marnie was the one holding Jake through the night while he cried.

The next morning, Jake felt as if he'd been hit by a semi. He ached all over, his eyes were swollen his throat raw and dry. He hadn't cried for Cassie in

JUST HOLD ON

more than eleven years. That first day, the day she died, he had cried and cried, but after that, he tried to be strong for his parents.

Then, his father left and Jake needed to be strong for his mother. He never cried for Cassie again, until last night. Once he started, he couldn't seem to stop. Today, he felt exhausted, but as if he'd released something inside him that had been festering for years, and he thought it might just be a good thing after all.

Jake knew Marnie must be wondering what happened to Cassie. He stood up, stretched his back, rubbed the back of his neck, then went into the kitchen to make some coffee. While that was brewing, he went to take a shower. He wished he could get the gritty feeling out of his eyes. It felt like he'd gotten sand in them. He let the hot water rush over him, pounding his aching muscles.

Once he got dressed and the coffee was done, he poured a cup and sat at the kitchen table, thinking. He would tell Marnie today. He shouldn't be holding back from telling her about Cassie. He wanted to be able to talk about Cassie with somebody, and he wanted someone besides him to be able to remember her. She deserved to be remembered. He heard Marnie stirring on the couch, waking up. He braced himself, readying his mind for the difficult conversation he knew would be coming.

~***~

Last night, Marnie wanted badly to comfort him, but didn't know how. She felt kind of bad, because she hadn't wanted to make him upset, she'd just wanted to give him a picture of him and Cassie together, because she knew he'd probably lost his photos in the fire.

Marnie walked into the kitchen and stared at Jake. He looked rough, almost ill. His eyes were really swollen, bloodshot. She sat down at the table and poured herself a cup of coffee.

Jake cleared his throat and then spoke, "Marnie, I—I want to thank you again, for the drawing. All the pictures I had of Cassie and me together were

JUST HOLD ON

lost in the fire, and they were probably the only things I had that really mattered to me. The picture you drew is really, really beautiful—it looks just like her. I'm going to frame it and hang it up, right out here in the living room, so I can see it every day..." He paused, cleared his throat again. "I know you probably wonder where Cassie is and I'm going to tell you what happened to her. It's hard for me to talk about. It's—very painful, but I'm going to tell you about her, because I want someone else to remember who she was." He swallowed another sip of his hot coffee.

They went back to the couch, Jake sitting on one end, Marnie's head in his lap. "When I was a kid, it seemed like all my friends had a brother or sister, but I didn't. Always wanted one, though. So, when my parents sat me down one night and told me they were having a baby, I was thrilled. Over the moon excited. I was eleven when they told me, and twelve by the time Cassie was born. I helped my dad paint the baby's bedroom and put the crib together. I thought I was going to die of anticipation but finally; the day came when the baby was born. My grandmother drove me up to the hospital, and I remember holding the baby in my arms. She seemed so little! I'd never held anything that small before, and I was just amazed by her. Once Mom came home with Cassie, I would spend hours holding her, watching her face and letting her hold my finger with her tiny fist. Of course, sometimes I got aggravated by her, when she would cry for hours on end and my mom couldn't get her to stop, but for the most part, I really enjoyed being a big brother..." He paused and looked away as if remembering the little baby.

Marnie lay on his lap and waited patiently for the rest.

"...When she got a little older, I would lay on her bedroom floor and play Lego's with her, showing her how to build a castle out of blocks. Once she was old enough, I let her climb up into my tree house and hang out with me and my friends. I ran alongside her when my dad took her training wheels off her bike to make sure she didn't fall down. As she got older it became apparent that she was a really talented athlete. Softball, basketball and soccer...basketball seemed to be her best sport. She was crazy good. By the time I was in the eleventh grade, I knew I wanted to be a teacher. I did well enough in college and was lucky enough to be able to do my student teaching at the middle school in my hometown...." He stopped again and looked all around the room as if he felt lost.

Marnie clenched her hands together and knew this may be hard for him to talk about...She figured she would just have to allow him to tell it in his own time.

"...Just as I was finishing that up, one of the older teachers decided to retire, and I was offered his job. I was so excited. I knew many of the teachers and families already, and had a good rapport with the kids. I felt like I was really living my dreams out. After a couple of years, Cassie was old enough to be in the middle school, and she loved that. It made her feel cool to be able to bring her friends down at lunch and eat in my classroom. One day, when she was thirteen, she——she was..."

At his halt, Marnie sat up, knowing something bad was to come in what he was about to say.

Jake stood up, cleared his throat, walked to kitchen, poured glass of Coke and came back to the couch. He rubbed at his eyes with his hand and swallowed hard. "One day, Cassie and her friends had come down to my room for lunch, and they were all sitting around, eating and teasing about boys, laughing at one another. Suddenly, I realized Cassie wasn't laughing. She was just sitting there, staring at me. I asked her what was wrong, and she didn't answer, her eyes just kept getting wider and wider. I stood up and asked again. She blinked and fell out of her seat. I told the other girls to go to the office and call 911. I knew what to do, because the school district required all the staff to take CPR classes every other year. My hands were shaking so hard, it was difficult to find her pulse. I put my ear down to her mouth and couldn't hear any breath sounds. I started compressions and gave breaths…"

Marnie held her breath and now, she did know now, how he must have felt when he tried to save Katie the same way.

"——she was lying there so still and quiet, her eyes wide open, her face so pale. I started yelling at

JUST HOLD ON

her to wake up and kept repeating the CPR. Finally, the paramedics came and took her away. I drove home and picked up my parents, then took the three of us to the hospital. The doctors didn't take us back to see Cassie. Instead, they took us to a small room that had a sign out front; *Counseling Room*. A doctor came in with us, shut the door behind himself and closed the window blinds." Jake stopped again and shook his head as he clasped his hands nervously together.

Marnie watched him closely, her heart breaking for him.

"It seemed like one half of my brain was thinking it knew what was coming, how this was very bad, while the other half was unable to comprehend what the guy was saying. My mom started screaming and my dad just sat there, saying nothing, doing nothing. I slid down the wall and covered my face with my hands. The doctor told us that Cassie was dead. Just like that—no sugar coating it—no trying to be nice for my mom's sake, he just said it flat out. 'Cassandra is dead. We think it was a sudden cardiac event of some kind. We'll know more if you let us autopsy. You and your family can stay here for an hour, then we need the room cleared.' He was such a jerk! So cold—hearted!" Jake's voice broke.

Marnie wanted to comfort him, take his hand…anything at all to help him.

"We were allowed to go look at her one last time. The room was a mess; a tube was still sticking out of her mouth, dried blood was caked around her lips. Her eyes were still open. Her clothes cut down the middle and pulled open. I wish I'd never gone to see her like that, because that's the picture of my sister that's always in my head when I think of her now. Anyway, I drove my parents home. I helped call family and friends to let them know. I called the school and told them I didn't know when I would be back, then helped my mom make funeral arrangements. That was—the hardest thing I have ever done in my life…"

A minute went by in silence, as she waited for him to continue.

"…The day after the funeral, my dad said he was going to the store for something—and he never

JUST HOLD ON

came back. He walked out on us, just like that. A few weeks later, he called and told my mom he couldn't handle it and wanted a divorce. My poor mom—she just fell apart. Quit going out, quit eating and started talking like Cassie was still alive. Said she could see Cassie, right there in the house, then she would say other really strange stuff. I took her to the doctor—to several doctors, for counseling. They gave her pills to take, but she seemed like she was getting more and more lost..."

Marnie could now see what happened to that poor woman she visited yesterday. She understood now.

"...She never got better, and the doctor told me she needed to be put in a home, so I found the nicest one I could afford. She doesn't even remember me anymore. I haven't heard from my dad since that last phone call he made to my mom. A few months after that, I broke up with Alexis, and that was that." He now stared at Marnie. "That's it. That's what happened to Cassie, and what happened to my mom, and—and what happened to me. I lost my entire family in just a few weeks time and I decided that loving people hurt too much, so I quit. I informed the school I wasn't coming back, found this freelancing job, so I rarely have to go to the office or meet with people, quit talking to my friends, quit Alexis and spent the next ten years living a very well-ordered and very lonely life—until the night of the fire." He reached out and grabbed Marnie's hands.

Startled, Marnie just stayed still and looked into his saddened eyes with her heart pounding furiously in her chest. *He's suffered the same way, he knows how I felt...* She squeezed his hands.

"Marnie, you're the first person I've talked with about this. And it hurts, it hurts a lot, but it feels— right. It feels good to be able to talk about Cassie. To know that you understand and care."

Marnie's heart hurt for Jake. How awful it must have been for him. His entire family had disintegrated in such a short time. No wonder, he felt so broken and cut himself off from everybody. She wished—she wished she could've been there for him to help him through that pain, the way he'd been here for her. She was so thankful for him. Such a

JUST HOLD ON

good person, so sweet with her and caring. Knowing how much he must be hurting made her feel like she wanted to take care of him and make *him* feel better. She crawled up beside Jake and wrapped her arms around him. It was all she could think of to do.

CHAPTER FOURTEEN

Jake kept thinking how irony could really be a bitch. Marnie was finally sleeping well through the night, and here he was, wide awake. *Again.* He felt as if his own body was betraying him. He'd already his mind made up that he would only see Marnie as his best friend and nothing more, but it seemed as if his body was constantly arguing that point with him.

For so many years, he'd turned off any feelings of desire, but sometimes lately, it felt like all the pent-up feelings from the last ten years were crashing down on him at once. Marnie was so beautiful, so precious to him, and it seemed to be a constant struggle now, to do what he knew was the right thing. He couldn't take advantage of her trust, or her vulnerability, but his growing attraction to her became difficult to keep in check. He told himself repeatedly, that he had to do this; he needed to control himself.

He stood up and went out to get a drink, then walked around in the living room. Running his fingers through his hair, he gave himself another pep talk. To make it seem stronger and more real, he said it out loud, "Get ahold of yourself, Jake! You *can* do this. You can control yourself now, the same way you have for the last ten years. You are an adult, too old to be getting swept away by fleeting emotions. You are in control! You are master of your own domain!"

Feeling better, although somewhat ridiculous, he sipped his Coke as he sat back against the couch. He knew he was right. It would absolutely be the wrong thing to do, to get involved with Marnie in a romantic sense. However, he couldn't deny the thought of a future with Marnie was appealing. It couldn't hurt to just daydream a little, could it? He wished they had met in different times, under different circumstances.

VALARIE SAVAGE KINNEY

The thought of proposing to Marnie made his blood run hot and he imagined what she would look like in a wedding dress, walking down an aisle to promise herself to him, forever. Jake imagined what it would be like, starting a family with her—and then he wondered if that would take away the pain in her eyes—the stark agony that was there, day in, day out.

A baby—would another baby make her happy? Another child certainly wouldn't take Katie's place, but it might ease the empty ache that Katie's death left in Marnie, and possibly a baby would ease the pain he still held inside from losing Cassie. Would that be so wrong?

While he considered the idea, he felt a little light headed. This fantasy was getting out of hand. He needed to stop thinking like this; it was just making everything more jumbled up in his head. He made his decision, and he had to stick with it. He and Marnie were best friends...he was her caregiver, not her lover. He would never, *could* never, be her lover. He knew what he was doing. He was going to stick with Marnie until she finished recovering, and then—and then what? He guessed then, he would have to leave. Get on with his life. A life without this woman, who turned his quiet and orderly world upside down.

The very thought of it pierced his heart and his breath caught in his chest. He was too much in love with—no, not *in* love with Marnie. Jake corrected himself; he didn't believe in that, right? He just loved her as a friend as—as a little sister and he loved her far too much to screw up their relationship. And then, maybe, once they were both doing better, and getting on with their own lives, they could hang out.

He might invite her over for dinner sometime. Exchange Christmas cards. *That would be good.* He didn't want her to be completely out of his life. He'd want to know how she was doing and besides, Barbossa would really miss her. *Yeah*, Jake let out a weak laugh. *The dog is really going to miss her.*

Finishing his drink, he dropped the glass in the sink and went back to bed. Turning resolutely away from Marnie, he shut his eyes tight and thought about anything other than feelings, sex, and women.

Especially, not the woman with the mesmerizing green eyes and gorgeous red hair, who was lying in bed just behind him. He didn't think about her at all…Not one bit.

~***~

Summer was over, and it became late enough into autumn that the leaves were dry and starting to fall from the trees.

Marnie felt agitated; Jake could tell. He didn't know what to do to help her. It did seem for awhile like Marnie was doing better. She still wasn't talking, but Jake had just about given up ever expecting her to do that. They managed just fine. If she needed to tell him something specific, she wrote it down.

Jake recently read Marnie a book about using hand signals to teach a dog tricks, and she had really taken to the idea, spending part of each day teaching Barbossa to lay down, roll over, and any other tricks

JUST HOLD ON

she thought he could manage with only one back leg. Days…weeks…months had gone by in quiet routine, but lately Jake noticed something was off.

Marnie paced in the apartment, reminding him of a caged animal. She gazed out the window, but seemed irritated when he offered to take her anywhere. She wasn't comfortable on the couch, or the bed, or even at the dining table. She quit board games halfway through, and couldn't sit still long enough to focus on any books he read to her. It seemed as if she was moving backwards in the recovery process.

Jake felt like he should know what to do to help her, but was helpless to know what she needed.

~***~

Marnie *was* feeling strange. She felt as though all the progress she made over the last few months had gone out the window, and she was powerless to stop it. Everything felt wrong to her. She had a headache all the time. She constantly felt tired and sluggish. Even her skin hurt—clothes and fabrics made her skin crawl. It was like having the 'flu, but it wasn't going away. She felt so *mad* all the time and she didn't even know why. It seemed as if just getting through the day, took every ounce of the meager energy she had.

Marnie often thought this must be what drowning felt like…treading water until, eventually, you just quit fighting and let the water cover you. The fact that scared her the most was she'd become so weary of treading water and was beginning to think it would be easier to stop fighting altogether.

~***~

Jake was in the kitchen, running water for dishes and cleaning up after dinner. He just remembered, he needed to call his boss and get his next assignment. He patted his jean pockets, looking for his cell phone, then remembered he had left it

JUST HOLD ON

sitting on top of the dresser in the bedroom. Singing softly to himself, he turned off the faucet and walked into the bedroom—and froze mid-step.

He hadn't realized Marnie had left the living room and gone into the bedroom to change into her pajamas.

There she stood, pajamas laid out on the bed, jeans and T-shirt in a puddle on the floor. She looked so startled; she just stood there, naked, looking at him.

"Ahh—I'm s-s-sorry—um..." Jake stammered. His brain was yelling at him to back up, get out of there, close his eyes—*anything* to block the vision of a nude Marnie from his mind, but stubbornly, his legs propelled him forward. NO! NO! *NO!* This was so wrong. He didn't *want* to do this—he *knew* he shouldn't be doing this. He felt like there was a disconnect between his brain and his body—his mind knew what he needed to do, but his body had completely opposite intentions. *And what was the deal with Marnie? Why the hell wasn't she covering herself up? What was she thinking, standing there naked, staring at him?*

VALARIE SAVAGE KINNEY

~***~

What *was* Marnie thinking? She just watched Jake walk towards her, watching his eyes heat up, looking at her with such desire it made her heart thud in her chest. She kept thinking she should reach for her clothes and say something— anything, to break the spell they both seemed to be under, but she was also thinking it felt good to be wanted—to feel like a woman worthy of desire and attention. It'd been so long since she felt that way. Over a year in fact.

First, Daniel had been called into action, and she tried to adjust to being without him, then he died, and she'd never had another chance to feel his arms around her, feel his lips on hers, or see desire for her burning in his eyes. She missed it—she missed being wanted.

It struck Marnie just recently how she existed completely without purpose. She was nobody's daughter, nobody's sister, nobody's

JUST HOLD ON

mother...nobody's wife. She had no title, little education and no job. She was worthless. Nothing—*less* than nothing. That's what she was thinking, standing there in the bedroom and waiting for Jake to reach her. That's what she was thinking when she felt Jake's arms on her bare shoulders, and felt his lips press against hers.

Marnie felt her body respond to his in a way she thought she would be embarrassed about, if she were in any other time, any other place. Right now, though, she knew only that she was wanted, needed and it felt so, so good. The fire that started low in her belly moved up, igniting her lungs until her breath came in ragged gasps, and finally the feeling lit her eyes with such intensity, she couldn't blink.

~***~

Jake's hands slid from Marnie's shoulders and into her hair, filling his fingers with the thick red tresses. His brain took snapshots as his eyes roamed across the parts of her body he'd never given himself permission to appreciate before.

Creamy white shoulders with a sprinkle of freckles spreading to her collarbone and the hollow in the center of her throat that begged his lips to press against it. His gaze drifted and his hand followed as he paused a moment to fully enjoy the weight of her soft breast in his hand and the sound of the sharp intake of breath that escaped from her lips when he touched her.

Jake's right hand was still tangled in her hair and he knotted his fingers more tightly into it until he almost—but not quite—jerked her head backward. His breath came in heavy spurts, and he sensed a warmth spreading through his body, not unlike the first heat of alcohol when it began to take effect. His eyelids were heavy, drowsy, but he fought to keep them open. He wanted to see every bit of her. His hand was exploring again—the dips between her ribs, the way her side caved in toward her belly and then the sharp ridge of her hip against his hand as it rested there for a moment.

JUST HOLD ON

Jake cupped one hand behind her neck, his other behind her knees, and lifted her feet off the floor. He stood still for a few minutes, taking the time to look at her beautiful body over again, and to give her a chance, if she wanted, to tell him "No, wait."

Marnie reached up to twirl a strand of his hair around her finger, and looked up at him. Her eyes were bright, gleaming, yearning. Her face looked flushed, so the splatters of freckles across her face darkened, each individual spot standing out like a bright star in a dark night sky.

The walk to the bed wasn't far—three steps, maybe four. Jake lowered Marnie onto the bed, and the buttons she had undone made it easy to slip his shirt off his shoulders. Feeling his bare chest against hers was nearly his undoing and he pressed against her, wanting more. He brushed some hair from her face, and murmured against her ear, "Let me make you feel good. Let me make you happy. I want to make you happy."

He could do this—he knew he could. Jake could make her forget everything else and just feel happy in this moment. He could make her smile…make her scream for him…beg for him.

CHAPTER FIFTEEN

Marnie arched against him. They were so close…only the barrier of Jake's shirt and jeans separated their bodies, and she wanted to know the feel of his skin against hers. She tugged at his shirt buttons and gazed up at his face, enjoying the effect she knew her body was having on him.

He kept breathing slowly, his hands moving deliberately across her body, inch by inch. Marnie felt alive. *Awake. Strong.*

His arms were strong, his grip was firm, and she enjoyed feeling safe, cradled in his arms this way. She bit her bottom lip with her front teeth, so hard, she tasted a little drop of blood, and she liked it. She wanted this—she wanted everything, every bit of him… right that second.

Marnie whimpered and pulled his face closer to hers, parting her lips to taste his mouth, his skin. She wrapped her legs around him, forcing his hips down, crushing against her smaller frame. No longer, was she thinking at all; her mind became filled with pure white heat, burning heat. The sensations boiling through her body made her feel as if she might explode if she couldn't get what she needed.

She stared directly into his eyes as she felt his chest, letting her fingers dance through the short black hair there, then over his hard stomach and finally the button of his jeans. Marnie felt a deep breath—a shudder—snake through his strong frame as she unzipped his zipper.

~***~

It felt so good; *she* felt so good, so perfect. It'd been too long since Jake had let himself fall this way…abandoning his lone-wolf-forever lifestyle and just enjoying the moment he was in. Marnie was so

JUST HOLD ON

beautiful, so soft and— she was kissing him back! His head was swimming with the burning heat of it, and he wanted it to go on and on—for it to never stop.

She kept touching him in ways he'd not felt in years, but his body reacted as if the last time had been just yesterday. He knew exactly what he wanted from her and exactly what he wanted to do to her. Jake could hardly believe Marnie wanted him this way, that she felt so eager and willing.

It was such an abrupt change from the broken, defeated girl she'd been just a short time ago, and he wondered if he was getting a glimpse of the woman she'd been before—before she had lost—

Before she lost her husband and daughter, and her home. Jake stopped—what was he doing? He rolled off of her and lay on his back on the bed, covering his eyes with his hands, drawing his knees up against the sickening, lurching feeling in his gut. *Oh, dear God.* He fought for control of his body and took a deep breath.

Marnie gazed over at him, hurt and looking confused. Tears welled in her eyes and threatened to spill over.

Jake felt like a monster. How could he have done such a thing? He was so angry at himself. He'd taken advantage of her—of *Marnie*! He promised her he wouldn't, and he'd just blown that promise out of the water. He ruined it—ruined *them* and whatever they'd been building together.

Marnie trusted him, and she was young and vulnerable— and he had taken advantage of her for his own benefit. He felt like he was going to throw up; he could taste a little vomit in the back of his throat.

Jake swallowed hard. He knew he could never undo the damage he'd probably done to their relationship. *Why, why do I always ruin everything?* "I'm—I'm sorry, Marnie. I shouldn't have done that. I'm so sorry. I—I need to get out of here for a little bit. Then—then when I get back, we'll talk about this. I didn't—I never wanted to hurt you. I want you—I want you so badly—but this just isn't right."

JUST HOLD ON

Jake yanked his shirt from the bed and slid it over his shoulders, put his shoes on, leashed the dog and headed outside for a long walk in the crisp autumn air. Running his fingers through his hair, he tried to calm his mind, gather his thoughts.

He felt so mad at himself his hands were shaking. He knew he needed to calm down, so he could go back home and say the right things to make up with Marnie—to let her know he loved her and wanted to keep their relationship strong and help her heal. He wouldn't try anything like that again. He would get himself under control—he knew he could do it.

~***~

Marnie felt lost and miserable. Worthless. Jake didn't want her—nobody else would either, she knew it. She hated her life, just *hated* it. There was nothing good in it anymore. Everything that was important to her was gone—everyone she loved was dead.

She walked into the bathroom, looking at herself in the mirror. A stranger looked back at her. *Who is this woman?* She reached up, touching her face. Her eyes were dull and lifeless, with dark purple circles under them. Her skin looked pale, her cheeks gaunt. Her hands fell to her belly,—flat and empty.

She suddenly remembered how it felt knowing Katie was growing within her. Sometimes, her stomach actually ached from losing Katie, as if Katie had never been born and had instead, been ripped directly away from her womb and died. The deep visceral pain in her gut would never leave—Marnie knew it would always haunt her,—hurt her.

Marnie's fingers traced the dark pinkish-purple stretch marks that striped her belly and hips. Once she'd hated those marks, hated the ugly scars they left on her skin. She felt the uneven groove of a particularly large streak, watching herself in the mirror as she ran her finger up and down, up and down, noting the puckering of her skin, the way

JUST HOLD ON

some of the marks had faded, while others seemed to have grown darker.

Now, these were some of the only external reminders that Katie had ever been real—that she ever existed. Marnie covered her breasts with her hands, remembering how different they felt when they were heavy with milk, swollen.

She stared into the mirror and could almost see Katie's round baby head resting in the crook of her arm, nursing, suckling contentedly. Closing her eyes, she imagined the way Katie's silken baby hair felt against her chest, the way a stray curl or two would stick to Katie's little face. Never would she see that again, or feel the weight of her baby in her arms.

Marnie opened her eyes, forcing herself back to the scrutiny of her own body. Touching her hair, she considered the length and color of it. Her hair had gotten so long, it hung past her waist. She picked a few strands up in her hand, studying it.

She's always kept her hair long at first, because her father insisted on it, then after he died her mother had her keep it long to honor his wishes.

Marnie had chosen to keep it long because of the notoriety it afforded her in high school. Red hair was rare enough at her school, and none of the other girls wore their hair long the way she did.

Daniel had loved her long, thick hair; he would gather it up in his hands and bury his face in it sometimes. When Katie was a baby, she would twist her tiny little fist into Marnie's hair and hold it when she nursed.

Some days though, Marnie got tired of dealing with such a heavy bunch of hair. It weighed her down, like an anchor and she was sick of it. In fact, she realized she'd never cut it shorter, because she wanted other people to like it. But she didn't like it—right at that moment— she really hated it. Hated the color, hated the length. She wished she could cut it off.

Well, she thought, *she could*. In fact, she would. She was going to cut it. Yes, that's exactly what she would do.

Whirling around, Marnie ran into the kitchen, rifling through drawers to find the scissors, getting angrier by the second. *Where are they?* She was sure

JUST HOLD ON

they had a pair somewhere. Scanning the kitchen, her eyes fell on the knife block. Grabbing a knife in her hand, she raced back to the bathroom and paused, for just a second.

Then, clutching a bunch of hair, she held it out from her head and started to cut. Sawing through her hair with that stupid knife felt GREAT—liberating, exciting. She grabbed another wad of hair and kept going, all the way around her head, then considered the effect her shorter hair had on her looks.

Marnie decided it wasn't short enough, so she started all over again. She wanted to look—no, she wanted to *be* completely different, someone new.

Her hair looked jagged, rough and now, only fell just below her chin. It suited her mood. Three feet of hair lay all over the floor and she felt a giddy rush from it, but it wasn't enough change. She craved more. Opening the bathroom cabinet, she grabbed the bottle of peroxide and opened it. Before she could change her mind, she bent her head over the sink and dumped the entire bottle into her hair.

She then, gazed up at herself in the mirror and wondered how long it would take to change from red to blonde. She'd never tried doing this before. She felt excited and realized, as she looked intently at herself that her eyes no longer looked lifeless. They were bright green, wide open, kind of frenzied looking and Marnie briefly wondered if she might be going crazy.

Then she decided, she didn't really care if she was or not. She felt thirsty suddenly, so she went out to the kitchen, and the hair she cut off clung to her legs and feet. She brushed at it, kicking it off herself and onto the kitchen floor. She took a glass down from the cupboard, filling it with cold water. She drained it quickly, then studied the glass in her hand.

Clear glass with little pink bows emblazoned across the top. She *hated* pink. She *hated* the stupid little bows. She *hated* everything! Pulling her arm back with all the force she could gather, she flung the stupid glass at the wall.

CRASH!

It felt so good. She opened the cupboard and grabbed two more – flung them at the wall, smashing into tiny bits of glass. Over and over, draining the shelf of all twelve of them. Her life

JUST HOLD ON

sucked. She would never be happy again, nothing was right. It wasn't fair! Why did all this happen to her?

She opened another cupboard, pulled out a plate. She'd been a *good* wife. She flung the plate at the wall. She'd been a *good* mother. *Smash!* Another plate. Unfaithful women got to keep their husbands. *Crash!* Negligent mothers got to keep their children. *Smash! Why? What had she ever done so wrong to deserve all of this misery? Crash!* She wanted her baby back! She want to watch Katie grow up, lose her baby teeth, learn to read.

Another plate dissolved into bits against the wall. She felt a strange sensation welling up inside her, traveling up from her belly, into her chest, then her throat. She opened her mouth, and listened in wonder to the strangled scream that erupted from her lips.

It felt good. She was sick and tired of being quiet. *No more!* She would scream when she wanted to, cry if she wanted to!

"AAAHHH!"Marnie screamed and screamed. "I hate this! I want my baby back! I want Daniel back! I want my life back!" She was so angry. All the months of silence and lethargy were over—she was mad as hell.

Oh, it hurt Marnie so much to say those words. Once they'd come out of her mouth and she heard them, she knew it was all real. There would be no more pretending; no more hoping it was all some awful nightmare; no covering it up with days at the beach and drawings, she scribbled out in the middle of the night. These terrible things had really happened.

She stomped out of the kitchen, cutting her bare feet on the slivers of glass that were all over the floor. She didn't care.

Out to the living room, she yanked the cushions off the couch, then shoved it until she flipped it upside down. With one swoop, she knocked all the DVD's off the shelf. Kicked the dining table chairs over. Flung the stack of library books off the end table. She didn't want to face a future without her husband and daughter. It was too hard, too awful, to look at the years ahead and know Daniel and Katie would never be with her again.

JUST HOLD ON

Slowly, she walked to the bathroom. Gingerly, she picked the knife up from the counter and looked herself in the mirror once more. Slowly, she pointed the knife at her wrist, closed her eyes, and pushed the blade into her skin.

Marnie opened her eyes and sucked in a deep breath. She watched with a strangely detached wonder as the dark red blood trailed down her forearm. Noted the stark contrast of the blood against her pale flesh. The pain wasn't as terrible as she imagined it might be and she felt an unexpected release of emotion as the blood welled up and began to gush in earnest.

Marnie blinked and twisted the knife tip just a little further. Looking down, she watched as the drips rolled from her arm and splattered across the cold white floor. Mesmerized, she watched as patterns emerged in the drops, the way they used to do when she and Katie watched fluffy white clouds in the summer sky. *This is right—fitting. The way it should be. Being left behind is too hard, and I can't do this; I can't. I want to die.*

She whispered it again, out loud, "I want to die. I want to die." *Didn't she?* She knew she wanted the pain to stop, the horrible emptiness to go away, but did she really want to die?

Daniel had loved life so much; he hadn't wanted to die and leave them. Katie had been a baby; she hadn't wanted to die. Marnie had the choice they hadn't been given. *Should she do it?*

Jake would be so hurt when he found her. He would be left alone again. What would this do to him? She shook her head and her thoughts began to clear. No, she didn't want to die. Not really. She just wanted not to be so miserable all the time. The knife clattered onto the bathroom tile. She pressed her thumb against the oozing, trying to stop the angry red flow.

Suddenly, the energy that had been fueling her rage—disappeared. Marnie collapsed into a heap on the floor, with great racking sobs shaking her entire body.

JUST HOLD ON

CHAPTER SIXTEEN

Jake was walking Barbossa through a public bike trail when his cell phone rang. *Who would be calling him?* He answered and was confused to hear his landlord asking if everything was okay.

"Yes," Jake replied, cautiously. "Why wouldn't it be?"

"Well," the landlord continued, "We've had some complaints from other tenants in the building about screams and sounds like something is breaking coming from your apartment. I wasn't sure if I should call the police?"

Jake immediately yanked Barbossa's leash and turned back to the opposite direction. "I'm on my way home. Just let me get back and see what's going on. If I need more help, I'll call." Jake started to jog, and when Barbossa couldn't keep up, he picked the little dog up into his arms and ran. *What had he done? Why had he left Marnie alone like that?* What kind of man was he? His breath was coming in short bursts, his chest burning.

Finally, he was home. He ran to open the door, dropping the dog, and then—he stopped. He blinked. What happened? What in the world was going on? Had they been robbed? Maybe he should have called the police before he just walked in. *What if Marnie had been hurt?* Oh, God, he would never forgive himself if— he could hear her crying. *Where was she?*

"Marnie? Marnie, are you hurt? Where are you?" Carefully, he walked through the maze of overturned furniture, following the sound of her sobs. Oh, dear God, there was blood. Trails of blood, all over the carpet.

There—there she was.

Jake hurried to her side, kneeling on the floor beside her. "What happened? Did someone break in? Did they hurt you? Where are you bleeding from?" Gathering her naked, crumpled form up into his arms, he blinked again. *What? Where was her hair? What had happened to it?*

JUST HOLD ON

He tried to make sense of the situation in his mind. They'd been robbed. She'd been hurt, somehow. And the burglars had—what? *Cut off her hair?* Now that he looked more closely, it wasn't just cut, it was a funny color. Like—streaked with a funny, brassy blonde color. What kind of robbers were they? Who *did* this? What would he tell the police? That they'd been robbed by the Hair-Chopping Bandits?

Cupping her face in his hands and wiping a few strands of strangely colored hair away from her face, he asked her again, what had happened.

Her mouth was working, open and shut, open and shut. Blood was smeared across her cheek. She stopped, swallowed, started again. "J-J—Jaaaake."

Finally, he was hearing his name coming from her lips. After ten months together, she was going to speak. Her voice was dry and hoarse, rusty from disuse. "J—Jaaaake."

"Yes, Marnie, tell me. Tell me what happened, let me fix it. I can make this better, just tell me baby."

She swallowed a sob, making an odd little strangling sound. "Jake—Katie died. She's dead, Jake. My baby is dead. She died in the fire. My baby, my baby, Jake—my baby is g-g-gone."

Jake felt utterly lost. Did she hit her head? He held her tightly against his chest. "Yes, honey. Yes, Katie died. Last January. But now, right now, are you hurt? Did someone hurt you?"

She stared into his eyes, working her mouth up to speak again. "And Daniel, too. Daniel died. He promised he would come back to me, but he didn't. He's dead. My Daniel is gone too, Jake. I can't bear living without them. I want—I want my family. I want my family back. I don't want to live without them."

Tears were streaming down her face, and as she covered her eyes with her hands, the tears mingled with the blood to turn a dirty pink.

When she brought her hands up, Jake saw the cut on her wrist, the crusted blood that covered her arm, and he grabbed it. "Marnie! What did you do? What have you done? Did you do this?"

JUST HOLD ON

Marnie couldn't respond—she was crying so hard. She sat up against the wall, pulling her knees up to her chest and dropping her head against her knees. She nodded her head slightly.

"Did you do..." He waved his arm in a sweeping motion "...all of this?"

Again, she nodded.

"Why?"

Marnie just shrugged her shoulders, continuing to weep.

"Marnie, I—I don't know what to do to help. I don't understand what's happening here." He waited—and waited.

Finally, he stood and, grabbing a cloth from the closet, he wet it and cleaned the wound on her wrist, covering it with ointment and a bandage, thanking God as he did so. Thankful, she hadn't pressed harder—hadn't actually hit a vein with the knife. Knowing the amount of blood he'd seen in the living room and hallway had to have come from more than just that one cut, he laid her limp form on the floor and checked her all over for injuries. Jake glanced up at her face and saw, with great sadness, how she was wearing the same blank, lifeless expression she'd worn the first few months they'd been together.

Had she completely regressed? Lost all the progress she'd fought for?

Finally—there was the problem. Her feet were cut and full of bits of glass. Jake sat on the bathroom floor and patiently picked each tiny piece of glass from her feet, then washed them and rubbed the ointment into them, tenderly wrapping them in bandages.

He picked her up and carried her to the bedroom, tucked her into bed, then set about cleaning the mess. He was stunned at the amount of shattered glass and broken shards from the plates she'd smashed. He couldn't imagine what had provoked her to do this kind of thing, or why she would suddenly become so destructive.

Jake thought it was probably his own fault, after what had happened earlier in the bedroom. He needed to apologize for that. And he was going to have to go do some shopping, because now they had nothing to drink out of or eat from.

JUST HOLD ON

He again, checked in on Marnie, and seeing that she was sleeping, he quietly got his shoes and coat on to run to the store to replace the dishes and glasses. He wondered if maybe this time, he should by all plastic. Just in case.

~***~

A week passed, and Jake was considering the idea that he may have to force Marnie into some kind of treatment to help her deal with Daniel and Katie's deaths. He didn't want to do it, but he really felt like he wasn't doing enough to help her. Jake wasn't sure if the fact that she was beginning to speak to him was a signal that she was improving, or not.

She finally cried and she kept on. In fact, that was just about all she did—cry, weep, lay in bed. Marnie barely left the bedroom all week, and she wasn't eating. When she wasn't in bed crying, she was on the floor, looking through her pictures, or drawing.

Jake tried talking to her, but she said she wanted to be left alone, so that's what he did.

Today, he'd just stepped out of the shower when he heard a strange sound coming from the living room. Toweling off, he cracked the door open and listened. *There it was again. Was Marnie out there, crying again?* She sounded—odd.

Pulling on his jeans, he walked down the hall and peered around the wall, assessing the situation. The TV was on, Marnie was on the couch and tears were streaming down her cheeks, but she wasn't crying, she was—laughing.

Laughing? Laughing!

Smiling through her tears, she gazed up at Jake and patted the couch next to her.

Jake sat, staring at Marnie in wonder. He'd never seen her laugh, or even smile like this before. What had changed? What was so funny? He glanced at the TV. Some guy was on cable, playing with puppets. It didn't look all that funny.

JUST HOLD ON

Looking back at him, Marnie wiped at her tears and giggled. "This guy is hysterical. He's my favorite comedian."

Jake had no idea who he was. "I've never seen him before."

"You've never watched Jeff Dunham? Are you serious, Jake?"

Jake felt excitement bubbling up in his chest. They were having a real conversation. "What makes this guy so funny to you?"

"He's a ventriloquist, Jake. He has a bunch of different characters and voices. Look,... See that one? That's Jose Jalapeño."

"And why, exactly, is that thing so funny?"

Marnie dissolved into another giggle fit. "Because! He's a talking jalapeno, and he's impaled on a stick."

"On a stick?"

"Exactly! Now you're getting it."

"Getting what?" Jake had no idea why she was laughing so hard, but he wanted to keep the conversation going. This was great. Better than great—awesome.

"*On a stick!*" she squealed. "That's the joke! *On a stick!*"

Jake stared intently into Marnie's face. Maybe this wasn't so great. He wondered briefly if she was having some kind of psychotic breakdown.

"Don't worry Jake, I'm not losing my mind. I'm not crazy. I can see by the look on your face that's what you're thinking, but I'm okay. I'm okay..." Marnie paused, took a deep breath, laced her fingers into his. "I'm *really* okay." She smiled up at him.

Jake brushed some hair away from her face. "I'm glad, honey, I really am. I've been really worried about you lately, especially after everything that happened a couple of weeks ago. Um—if you feel like talking, I have a few things I would like to say." He waited a few seconds.

Marnie nodded at him.

He took her hands in his and shifted, so he knelt directly in front of her. "I want to apologize to you for what happened, um, in—in the bedroom, the day I walked in on you. I'm sorry. I let myself get out of hand, after I promised you that I wouldn't. I can't

JUST HOLD ON

excuse myself, but I want to explain that—I mean, it's not that..." Frustrated, Jake ran a hand through his hair, and started again, "It's hard for me to talk about things like this. I'm not good at it. Okay, so here's the thing. You know—I mean, you know about Alexis; I told you about her. Well, since then—I mean since I broke up with Alexis, I haven't been with anybody. I mean, I haven't been with any women."

She sat quietly and stared at his face.

Jake thought it didn't sound quite right. "Or men." *Oh God, that sounded even worse!* "Not that I *would* be with a man. Not that—okay, this isn't coming out right, Marnie." He stopped and took a deep breath. Then, let it out slowly. "What I want to say is, I've been lonely for a really long time." Jake thought for a moment. "It's been almost eleven years since I broke up with Alexis, and I haven't dated anyone since then. I don't think I realized how lonely my life had become until I found you. It's like I—it's like I just shoved all those feelings down inside and ignored them..." He squeezed her hands and paused.

"...And it became really easy to do, when there were no beautiful women around to stir those feelings up. But now, I do—now, I do have a really beautiful woman around, and you are—God, Marnie, I don't know if you even realize how incredibly attractive you are. And when I walked in on you, just standing there like that, it felt like all those feelings from the past eleven years just overwhelmed me, all in one rush, and I just totally lost control of myself. But I shouldn't have, and I feel responsible for hurting you, and then you were so upset...." He sighed.

Marnie shook her head at him.

"...And then, when landlord called me and I thought someone had broken in here and hurt you, and I thought I would just die—just *die*, if you were hurt. I can't imagine living without you, Marnie. And I just wanted to say I'm sorry for hurting you, for taking advantage of you and for making you upset. It scared the life out of me, thinking you were hurt, and then seeing you there, bleeding, and how you had cut yourself. I feel responsible for that, too. Please, please, don't ever do that again, Marnie!

JUST HOLD ON

Don't hurt yourself like that. I need you here with me, because you are my best friend, and you are so beautiful to me and—I need you, and—Marnie…" He tipped her chin up, so that their eyes met, and swallowed hard.

Her eyes widened as she listened to his ranting.

"I—I love you, Marnie. *Please* don't ever try to hurt yourself like that again? I promise, I won't try anything with you. I could even start sleeping out here on the couch if it would make you feel better."

Jake knew he needed to stop talking, he was so out of breath. He sat back, hoping she understood what he'd been trying to say. He'd never been very good at expressing emotions, and he'd even gotten worse at it, because he hadn't talked to anyone for so long.

Marnie's stunned expression gradually softened.

Jake released a breath. *Maybe she will forgive me and maybe, she understands.*

CHAPTER SEVENTEEN

Marnie suddenly felt so bad about how he'd been feeling guilty all this time, when her actions that night actually had very little to do with him. "Jake, listen to me. Really listen. I don't want you feeling guilty about that night. I am an adult, okay? I'm not a child and I played just as much of a role in what happened as you did. I understand what you are saying too, about being lonely that way. It's hard, I know. I've been feeling the same way. Sometimes, I really miss being Daniel's wife. I mean—well you know what I mean, in the sense that…"

Jake tilted his head as though he didn't understand.

JUST HOLD ON

Marnie could feel her face reddening. "I miss feeling *wanted* by him. In that way. To feel—that I'm desirable, I guess. It's been so long since...." Her voice trailed off for a minute. "I miss that part of my life. I mean, I'm not a child, and I'm not a nun—I want, I mean I miss—doing that. Being close like that with someone." She leaned her head onto Jake's shoulder.

He wrapped his arms securely around her.

"I feel lost, Jake. Who am I? Who am I if I'm not Daniel's wife? If I'm not Katie's mother? I keep thinking about that. I'm starting to get through the grief, I think. I feel better than I have in a long, long time. I think—I think I can accept that they are gone. It's so hard! I want to look ahead, but—I just can't imagine a future without them in it. Without the three of us together. Without—without my husband and my daughter, I'm not anyone. I'm just useless. I don't have a job. I never went to college." Marnie paused again.

Jake's eyes filled with tears as he pulled away to look at her.

"Anyway, that's what I'd been thinking about, that night when you came in. And I'm not proud of myself for just standing there and letting all that happen. I'm not that kind of person. It just felt good to see that—that you wanted me, in that way. The way you were looking at me, it made me feel attractive. *Wanted.* But I shouldn't have done that, so I'm sorry too. It wasn't all you, Jake. Remember, I kissed you back. And I want you to know that for weeks now, I've felt different…" She grew quiet for another minute or so.

Jake just held her and comforted her, just like he always did.

"…All the pent-up emotions from the last year have been bubbling to the surface and I haven't known how to deal with them. You and I are alike in a lot of ways, I think, Jake. I haven't known how to handle these feelings, so I've kept them deep inside. I guess, kind of hoping they would just go away. I mean, I think in another way, I just couldn't handle the emotions, so my brain kind of turned off for a long time. Without you, I wouldn't have made it. You took care of me—you moved in with me—

geez, you even cleaned up the mess whenever I threw up! You are a good man, Jake, and—and because of that, I love you too." She smiled up at him, and they sat that way for a long while, in silence.

"Jake, I've never thanked you for trying so hard to save Katie. I know you did all you could. It's not your fault, you know? That—that she didn't make it. They told me at the hospital that she died from smoke inhalation, probably before we'd even gotten her out of the apartment. Her death had nothing to do with what you did or didn't do. I want to ask you something, Jake. I just—crap, I'm going to start crying again!" She wiped her eyes and waited a moment. "I've been wanting to ask you—just—why? Why, did you do all this for me? You didn't even know me back then. You risked your life for me and Katie, and now you've given up almost a whole year of your life, taking care of me. I guess I just wondered why you did.""I don't know, Marnie. It just seemed like the right thing to do. I mean, I knew you guys were in the apartment, the fire was getting worse, and there was no one else in sight who could come and help. What else would I do? Just walk out and not even try to help you? I guess after that, I thought that you needed help. I felt sorry for you and it seemed like you were all alone. I'd been feeling, for a long time that I needed to break out of my sheltered, lonely life and connect with someone again...." He halted and looked into her eyes.

They sat for a moment as both of them swiped at their tears.

"...I just couldn't remember how to connect. I'm not—not really very good with people anymore. I just—I don't know. I wanted to. I really did. I wanted to take care of you, make sure you were okay. I thought—I thought if Cassie had ever been in this situation, I would want someone to step in and help her out."

"Is that how you see me, Jake? Do you see me as a little sister?"

"Um—at first, maybe I guess I did. You're so young and vulnerable. Why? Does that bother you?"

"I'm not that young, Jake. I doubt I'm much younger than you."

JUST HOLD ON

He laughed. "Yeah right, Marnie. What are you? Maybe 23?"

"I'll be 30 in December."

Jake shook his head in disbelief. "You will not. There's no way."

"I'm pretty sure, I know my own age, Jake. People often take me for younger because of the way I'm built, but just because I'm short, doesn't mean I don't get another year older every year, like everyone else."

"This is a weird reason to get mad at me, Marnie."

She sighed. "I'm not mad at you, Jake. I'm just mad…at everything. And sad. Sometimes, happy. I'm working on dealing with my feelings, instead of hiding from them, but some days, I have such a rush of different emotions at once, I don't even know what to do with myself."

"Maybe…have you thought of maybe talking to someone? A counselor?"

"Actually, I think I'm getting better. Better than I have been in the last year, anyway. I can talk now. I can cry, I can eat. As long as you let me talk to you, I think I will be okay. I mean—I don't think I will ever go back to being the person I was before…before losing Daniel and Katie. I think there will always be a part of me that feels such a searing pain at that loss; part of me will always have that hole that no one else can fill…" She paused to stare off.

Jake simply continued to hold her hands in his.

"It's going to take me a long time. Sometimes, Jake, I feel like I'm really making progress and on other days, I feel like it's one step forward, ten steps back, you know? But, I mean, now that my head is getting more clear, I've been thinking that—that I can't keep letting you support me. It isn't right. You should be able to get on with your life."

"My *life*? What life?" Jake asked in a loud voice, which wasn't usual for him. "Working from home, having no friends, spending all my time alone? I don't mind paying the rent here; I have to pay rent wherever I live, anyway. At least here, I have someone else around, someone to talk to—unless you *want* me to leave. Do you?"

JUST HOLD ON

"No! Jake, it's not that I want you to leave—I don't. I just feel like you're wasting your life on me. You've spent almost a year, sitting in this apartment with me. I don't want to hold you back from whatever else you want to do. And I feel—I don't know— kind of guilty, I guess. Like, I'm not contributing anything at all."

Jake looked as if he pondered something for a long moment, then cleared his throat. "That's what I think you don't understand, Marnie. You *have* contributed. I've needed you, just as much as you've needed me. Being with you has changed me…brought me friendship…helped me to open up and feel again. I can't imagine not being with you, but I understand what you're saying. I don't want to hold you back, either. I hope someday, you have a great life, meet some wonderful guy and maybe have a houseful of kids. I can visit at Christmas and be their old Uncle Jake."

"I don't want to meet anyone else. I want to stay here—with you."

"Marnie, I know you don't want to hear this, but sometime, you're going to have to leave this apartment—and I don't just mean to go sit at the waterfront with me and the dog. You should have friends, go out…have fun. You need to start driving again, run errands on your own. You know what I mean?"

Marnie fell silent for a long while, thinking. "I know that. Do you think I don't know that? I do know, but I don't want to—go out there." She waved her hand toward the window. "I don't want to because—if—when I do, people will talk to me, and sooner or later, they'll know what happened, and then they'll say things to me. Awful, terrible things, and I just can't stand it. I can't stand it, Jake! Because I know what they will say…I've heard it all before. Stupid, hateful platitudes that I've heard a million times."

Jake shook his head at her.

"When my mother died. When Daniel died. Those people…they have *no idea* what I've been through, and they say things like, 'You'll get over it soon' or 'You'll feel all better in three months', or six months, or a year, or whatever stupid timetable they throw out there. As if, when that magical date comes around, everything will be just fine, and my life will be perfect again. Well, I have news for them! You don't 'get over it'…EVER! I can't—I can't get over it. I will never get over it. Never, Jake. Never."

Jake looked troubled as he watched her.

Marnie stood up and walked over to the window. "And do you know what else? You know what else, Jake? I am so mad at those people, because their lives just go on. They keep moving through their days, like it doesn't even matter. And it should matter." Marnie stopped and pressed her hand to her chest, clutching a fistful of her shirt. "My loss should *matter*, Jake. I want those people to stop enjoying the weather that my daughter will never play outside in. I want them to close the schools that my daughter will never attend. I want them to lock up the parks Katie will never play at…and I want the world—all of it, all of them—to stop and mourn with me. My world stopped that day and their lives should have stopped too."

Jake bit at his lip, as if he knew her pain and he actually felt it.

"It makes me angry, really angry Jake, that their lives keep moving on as if Katie was never in this world—as if losing her didn't change the world at all. But it did. It *should*. And some days, some days Jake, I feel so mad. I think if I go out there on the streets with them, or into stores or restaurants or the movie theater with them, I'm going to snap. I'll just...scream. Choke some random person, or hit someone with the car, because—because I want them to see! I want them to notice. I'm scared of myself—of what I might do. And that's why...that's why it's better if I just stay inside."

"Okay."

"Okay? *Okay*? I'm pouring my heart out to you, and that's all you can say? Okay?"

"Okay. Okay, Marnie, I understand what you are saying. Okay, it makes sense to me. I have felt that way since losing Cassie too. You have a right to be angry. You've been through some really awful experiences. You can stay inside until you are ready to go out there. I'm glad you are finally telling me how you feel. Okay. Okay."

JUST HOLD ON

Marnie wiped at her tears, gulped down a sob as it escaped her lips. "Jake? I don't think I'm ever going to be normal again." Her voice dropped low.

Jake stood and walked over to where she stood. He wrapped his arms around her, and rested his chin on her shoulder, watching out the window with her. "I know. But hey, normal is just a cycle on a washing machine, right? Marnie, remember that you can't rush grief. Look at how long I've been screwed up. I can look back and wish I hadn't lost all those years, grieving and isolating myself, but I can't undo what has been done. I can only go forward. Same with you. Someday, Marnie, you'll be ready to start moving forward. And as long as you want me here, I'll be here. I'll stay with you, and be here for you, as long as you need me, as long as you want me. I'm not going anywhere."

CHAPTER EIGHTEEN

Thanksgiving was coming up soon, which would be the first holiday Jake and Marnie spent celebrated together. Other holidays had come and gone, certainly, but those days slipped by, unnoticed.

Jake felt kind of excited to be having a regular Thanksgiving dinner and someone to share it with. He'd been planning the menu for a couple of weeks now, printing out recipes he'd found online and purchasing groceries with anticipation. He intended to go all out for the special day and even bought some decorations, sprucing the apartment up with tiny gourds, hanging cut outs of turkeys and pilgrims. Hanging the decorations up, brought feelings of nostalgia and reminded Jake of when he'd been teaching and would decorate his

JUST HOLD ON

classroom for each holiday during the school year. Sometimes, he really missed teaching…missed feeling as though he was making an impact in children's lives.

Then, Jake watched as Marnie washed dishes, humming to herself. She'd been in such a good mood lately, and he wondered why. The last few days he hadn't seen her crying at all. She was cheerful and talkative, energetic and busy. It's not that he wasn't happy about the change, he was just curious as to what had brought it about. He didn't want to ask and somehow spoil it, so he decided to enjoy it while it lasted.

~***~

Marnie did have mixed feelings about the upcoming holiday. Jake seemed so excited and she thought it was sweet the way he took it all so seriously. She'd been helping him choose recipes, which reminded her of when she was small and would help her mother get ready for Thanksgiving.

It'd been Marnie's job to spend the day before the holiday, tearing up loaves of bread into tiny bits for the turkey stuffing. Of course, she also helped her mom with the baking and she remembered how she really enjoyed rolling out dough for the pies. Marnie had planned to teach Katie how to do those things…

She shook her head and forced herself to focus on something else. This is where the mixed feelings came in—it had been easier when she and Jake ignored the holidays and let them pass by without mention. It would be so hard to celebrate a time like this without being assaulted by memories. At the same time, Marnie knew there would be hundreds of holidays in the next few years and she needed to find a way to get through them.

Jake just left to go visit his mother. Marnie had never gone to visit his mom again. She would have, but it seemed to upset his mom so much the last time. She helped Jake bake some pies to take to the home to share with the residents and staff.

JUST HOLD ON

Bored, Marnie flipped the TV on and curled up on the couch with Barbossa. Nothing interesting was on. She stood and walked over to the window. Looking outside, she wished she could make herself go out there. Sooner or later, she knew she would have to force herself to do it. She couldn't stay in this apartment forever, wasting her life, watching TV and listening to Jake read her books.

They hadn't been to the waterfront in a couple of months, not since the weather had gotten so much colder. This left Marnie feeling antsy from being cooped up inside, but she dreaded going out into the crowds, having to talk to people, having to explain about Daniel and Katie. Maybe…maybe after the first of the year, she would do it. That could be her resolution for New Year's, going to a store or something.

Grabbing a box of treats, she sat on the floor with Barbossa to do some training. They were still working on rolling over. Waving the treat in a circle, she coached him to do it. "Roll over, roll over, c'mon sweetie, roll over."

He rolled onto his back and stopped—this is as far as he ever got.

Marnie sighed. "Alright, let's take a break." Leaning against the couch, she picked up the remote and started flipping channels again. *When would Jake get back? He was taking forever.* She heard a cooing baby and glanced back up at the TV screen.

A commercial for baby diapers was showing, and Marnie stared at the screen, mesmerized. The baby looked so sweet—so little. Such precious sparkling blue eyes. She wished she could reach right into the screen and pull that baby out, hold him, plant a light kiss on his forehead. Rock him to sleep.

Marnie reached out, touching the screen with her finger. She traced the tiny mouth, formed into a perfect 'O'. She ran her finger over the curls that sprang from the baby's head. Oh, how her heart ached for her lost baby. Her chest hurt with actual pain. She let herself remember how Katie had been at that age. If only, she could have that time back, she would have slept less, wasted less time doing

JUST HOLD ON

pointless chores and worrying about how to lose that last ten pounds of baby weight.

She would have held Katie all day long, relishing every second the way a starving man would cherish a drop of water or slice of bread. She would have taken more pictures and written more little moments down in a journal. She would have drawn Katie more often; every precious bit of her, from her wispy blonde curls to her tiny little toes.

Marnie held her stomach and bent over on the floor. She thought she might throw up. She closed her eyes and took deep breaths, trying to calm her body down. She wished Jake were here—he would hold her against him, tell her it would be okay. He would sing to her until her breathing settled down and her stomach stopped flipping over. It was no use, she could feel it coming—she ran to the bathroom just in time and lost the little bit of breakfast she'd eaten today. *When would this stop? When would it be safe to casually watch TV, or listen to the radio, without some simple commercial or song triggering her grief this way? Would she ever feel like herself again?*

VALARIE SAVAGE KINNEY

Marnie couldn't get that stupid diaper commercial out of her head. The baby reminded her so much of Katie. No matter how hard she tried, she couldn't seem to move past the empty ache in her gut, the constant need to hold her daughter again. She felt like grief covered every part of her, sticking to her like a second skin, she could never shake off. Marnie loved being a mother, loved caring for her little girl and watching her sleep at night. She wanted her back so badly—she *needed* her back. She needed to be a mother again, she needed her own baby to hold in her arms…Her baby.

Marnie stopped, thought about it for a second. A baby—she could have another baby, she was still young. The thought bounced around in her brain for a few minutes. The more she thought about it, the more it made sense to her. This, *this* is what she needed. This is why she felt so restless, so lost. She needed a baby to anchor her, to give her a reason…a purpose to wake up in the morning.

Her growing excitement became difficult to contain. She felt certain Jake would be willing. He would make a wonderful father. It would be good for

JUST HOLD ON

both of them—heal both of them of their sadness, their losses. *It was perfect!* She didn't know why she hadn't thought of this before. She would need to present the idea to him in just the right way.

This was so exciting. A baby! Marnie couldn't wait to be a mother again. She smiled to herself. *This was it, this was exactly what she needed to make everything better.*

~***~

The table was set along with two tall white candles lit. Jake already carved the turkey and set the slices on a platter in the center of the table. The carved meat sat while surrounded by heaping bowls of mashed potatoes, stuffing, cranberries (the real kind, not the gelled cylinder from a can). A green bean casserole, flaky biscuits, homemade gravy and tossed salad. In fact, there seemed to be so much food and the table was so tiny, Jake felt afraid to rest even his elbows on the edge for fear he would knock something off.

The kitchen counter also looked quite overwhelmed: four different flavors of pie, two cakes, a pumpkin and cream cheese roll, three cans of whipping cream and some odd concoction Marnie had tossed together, involving blueberry pie filling, canned pineapple, evaporated milk and Cool whip.

Jake and Marnie sat across from each other, eyeing the bounty of food before them and warily considering how much of it they could possibly consume.

"It really didn't seem like it was that much. I mean, while I was making it," Jake noted.

Marnie cleared her throat. "It's fine. It's—great. Everything looks so good. I didn't know you knew how to make all this stuff. You did a great job. I'm...really hungry. Really hungry." She swallowed, took another spoonful of mashed potatoes. "So, listen—I wanted to talk to you about something, Jake." She twirled her fork on her plate, dragging it so it made four perfectly even little paths through the potatoes.

JUST HOLD ON

Jake filled his fork, stabbing some turkey first, then some stuffing, green beans and finally, a little dip of mashed potatoes. He shoved the fork into his mouth, chewing as he looked at her.

Marnie kept smiling, but looked a little bit anxious.

He nodded in encouragement—*what is this about?*

She tucked her hair behind her ear and cleared her throat again.

Jake waited, filled his fork up again, brought it halfway back to his mouth...

"I think we should have a baby together."

Jake froze, fork midair. The mountain of food he just started to swallow stuck in his throat.

"I've been thinking about this for a while, Jake. I think it would be good for us, *both* of us. I think we would be really good together. You would be a great father, I just know it."

Suddenly, Jake's mouth went dry—so dry. He tried again to swallow the lump of congealed Thanksgiving goodness trapped in his throat, but it didn't move. His fork was still poised in the air, with his mouth hanging open and his eyes wide, he probably resembled an infant whose mother was trying to tempt him into eating by playing 'Airplane' with the food.

Oblivious to his plight, Marnie began ticking off her list of *'Reasons Why Having a Baby Would Fix Everything'*. "This last year has been so negative, Jake. A baby would be a positive, something to look forward to. I'm not getting any younger and to be honest, neither are you. If I'm going to be a mother again, I can't keep waiting, because I might want more than one. Neither of us really has any family left, so why not start our own? I think it would help heal us, both of us Jake, to have a baby. It would knock you out of your shell, help get you past Cassie's death.." She paused to stare at him.

Jake still sat frozen like a statue.

"...And it would help me too. I know it would, Jake. It would help me get past losing—well, you know, losing Katie and everything. I need this...I *need* this. I need a baby. I need to know that somebody needs me. Depends on me. That's what I need in my life to—to be happy. This would make *us* happy. This is what we need to make us happy, Jake. I really think we should do it." Marnie finally wound her speech down.

All Jake could do was to stare at her…

CHAPTER NINETEEN

It was funny—in her head this speech sounded so much more eloquent, more persuasive. She finished with a whispered, "Please" Then took a deep breath and gazed up to meet Jake's eyes.

Crap. He didn't look as happy as she hoped he would. He looked—rather awful. Panicked, even. Did he hate the idea of starting a family with her so much? Geez, he looked *so* stricken. She felt anger rising up in her throat. "You don't have to look so panicked, Jake. For crying out loud. I would have thought you'd be happy about this. You yourself said it had been at least ten years since you've gone to bed with…" Marnie halted and really looked at Jake.

What is wrong with him?

JUST HOLD ON

The hand holding his fork midair was shaking, his eyes were wide, bloodshot, blinking. His mouth opened and shut, opened and shut. Was he choking?

Oh, God! She jumped out of her chair, knocking it over as she stumbled to the other side of the table. She grabbed him by the shoulders, turned him toward her. "Jake? Are you choking?"

He blinked.

"What should I do? I don't know what to do!"

Jake blinked again.

Marnie grabbed his arm, holding it high above his head, shaking it. She wasn't sure that would help, but it was what her mother used to do if she saw someone choking. It didn't seem to be helping.

This is happening, Marnie thought, *this is actually happening to me again. I'm going to lose him; I'm going to lose Jake!* Anxiety clenched her chest with a sickening pain. She grabbed his other arm, holding both of them up and shaking them harder. She looked back at Jake; he was turning very red. *No, no, no!* She wasn't going to let this happen.

"Jake? What should I do? Should I call 911? I don't know what to do!" Helplessly, Marnie looked around the apartment as if the answer would magically materialize. She knew she wasn't thinking straight. *Think Marnie, think. Think.* She stopped, dropped his hands and tried to think.

Jake took her hand in his, made a fist with it and placed it near his sternum, making a pushing motion. *Oh, right! Yes.* Marnie remembered having seen that on TV before. What was that called? Heimlich maneuver.

She quickly stepped behind Jake, placing both fists into the groove just below his rib cage, and shoving as hard as she could. Nothing. She did it again, and a horrifically large chunk of food shot out of Jake's mouth and landed on the floor.

Marnie winced at the loud whistle Jake made as he started gasping for air. She felt like she should do something else for him, but wasn't sure what, so she went and got him a glass of water. When she came back, Jake had his arms on the table with his head resting on them.

He still seemed to be breathing heavily, shuddering.

JUST HOLD ON

Marnie sat the glass on the table and pulled a chair over, so she could sit next to him. She stacked some of the dishes to make a little bit more room, then reached over and rubbed his back. Wow, so much for her big idea. She'd been so gung ho and focused on convincing him to agree with her, she's almost killed him. *Smart move, Marnie.*

"Marnie?" Jake's voice came out as little more than a hoarse whisper, "Just give me a couple minutes, and then we can talk about—about—what you were saying. Okay?" He sat up and took a small sip of water then leaned back in his chair and closed his eyes again.

Marnie's heart was still pounding. That whole experience had been so scary. What if she hadn't been able to help him? What would she have done if she'd lost him? The very thought of it made her feel sick.

A little while later, he called out for her, "Marnie?" Jake was sitting on the couch, and patted the empty space next to him in invitation. "Come here, I want to talk to you."

Marnie slowly walked across the living room and sat down, but kept her eyes averted. She wanted to beg and plead her case with him, but she kind of felt embarrassed now, after the drama of him choking and everything.

They sat quietly together for a while. After a few minutes, Jake reached out to hold her hand. He cleared his throat, then spoke thoughtfully, seeming to choose his words with care. "Marnie, I want you to know that I—I hear you, and I understand what you are saying. I understand why you want another baby. I'm not mad or anything, and I'm not even totally opposed to the idea. I mean, I can see the merit, and I love kids, I really do. And I—I love *you*, Marnie. I'd be lying if I said I have never entertained thoughts of you and me—um together, you know, in that way. Um, I am surprised because, well, I'm just surprised that you would bring this topic up, and I think I need a while to think about it."

Marnie's eyes remained downcast.

"Marnie. Marnie? Look at me." Jake took her chin in his hand and gently lifted it upward. He took a deep breath. "Marnie, listen. I think over the last year or so, we've both changed a lot. I mean, we've been through a lot together, and I think we are both beginning to come out on the other side of that darkness. Coming out stronger, better. You've come *so far*. Sometimes, I wonder if you realize just how far you've come. It amazes me. I'm so proud of you. I know, without a doubt, that you would be a fantastic mother, Marnie. I know that. And I think I could be a decent dad. And we—I mean, honestly, if we've survived what we've been through in the last year and still have a relationship, I think we can probably get through anything, but I think it would be wrong, at this point, to add another person to the mix."

Marnie opened her mouth in protest, and Jake held up his hand. "Wait, wait. Just hear me out, listen to me for a minute. We both have a long ways to go, Marnie. Someday? Maybe. But right now? Think about it for a few minutes here. What about doctor appointments? And after a baby is here, what then? You'd have to take the child to the doctor, playdates, preschool. Honey, you can hardly get from the door to the car. You haven't been inside a store in almost a full year. You haven't spoken to anyone besides me. And I'm still working through my own issues."

Jake watched as Marnie's eyes filled with tears, and a lone tear drop snaked down her cheek. He wiped it away with his thumb, brushed the hair from her face and tucked it behind her ear. "I'm not saying it won't happen, I just don't think right now is a good time. Do you understand what I'm saying? And I think we really need to discuss what we want from a relationship with each other. Are we going to remain friends, or do we both want something more? Because, Marnie, if this is something you really want to do, then I want it to be for the long haul. I don't want you to change your mind in a year or two, or suddenly realize a few years down the road that you're only with me out of convenience, because I was the one who was there."

Marnie fell silent for a few moments. "I really wanted this, Jake. I really want this."

"I know you do. I know, but you—well, both of us, we both need to be healthier, stronger, before we can make this decision. We need to be able to provide a good, stable home for a child. Do you understand what I'm saying?"

Marnie sniffled, nodded.

"It would be easy for us to think that having a baby would fix everything that's wrong with us now, but would that be fair to the kid? I mean, part of being good parents is being unselfish. And doing this now, Marnie, doing this now would be really selfish on our part." Jake shifted slightly, turned so he could pull Marnie back against him and wrapped his arms around her.

She relaxed just a little bit, leaned her head back to rest on his chest.

"Something else I want to talk about, Marnie. I didn't want to bring this up just now, but I think I need to, because it's only fair for you to know where I stand on the subject. Marnie, I don't...." Jake paused, considering how to explain himself. "I don't want to—I mean, I've never wanted to—ahh, damn this isn't coming out right. I guess I just want to be clear about this. Marnie, when my dad left it had a huge impact on me. I was an adult, not even living at home anymore, but it really hit me hard. I think I could have gotten through Cassie's death, or at least done better dealing with losing her, if he hadn't left. I don't know if we are even at a place in this...relationship of ours where I should bring this up..." he halted again, to take a deep breath.

Marine sat very still in his arms.

"...And I don't want to scare you or anything, but Marnie, if we really are considering this—this change in our relationship, then you need to know that I'm not messing around. If we're going to talk about having a child together, then first we need to talk about—okay, about marriage. Not that I'm proposing that right now. Well, not that I'm against it, either."

Jake stopped talking again, while feeling frustrated. This wasn't coming out right at all. "I guess what I want to say, Marnie, is that I want the whole deal. All of it. I want to know I have a solid marriage and yes, kids and a house, and—and I want stability. Permanence. I don't want ever, *ever* to put a child through what I went through when my parents split up. If we're going to talk about this, I mean us, as in *us staying together*, seeing what we

JUST HOLD ON

can build together, then you need to know I'm serious. I'm talking about a lifetime, and I am not going to take that lightly. So, if you're not thinking along those same lines, then—then we probably shouldn't continue this conversation." Whew, Jake's throat felt dry. He glanced at the clock to realize he'd been talking a long time.

Marnie hadn't said a word ever since he started.

He peered down at her and tipped her face up, so she could meet his eyes. "Marnie? I don't want an answer right now, because I think we both need to spend some time thinking about this, and about what we want, but you should know that I—well, honestly Marnie, I've spent enough time alone and if we decide to do this, to take this step, I'm going to need to know that you want *me*. That you're in love with *me*. I'm not—I won't be a replacement for Daniel, stepping into the hole he left. I'm not interested in being the rebound guy, or just because it's convenient for us to be together. I don't give my heart away lightly. I don't want it broken again, Marnie. I couldn't take it. I can't do it. Can you understand that?" Jake glanced down at her again.

Great...just great. He was bearing his soul to her, and she'd fallen asleep.

Jake watched her for a few minutes. She looked so beautiful, even with her hair hacked off unevenly and looking at her now, his breath caught in his chest. He planted a light kiss on the top of her head, and whispered softly, "Don't break my heart, Marnie. Please don't break my heart. I love you so much."

He pulled a throw pillow from the center of the couch, tucked it behind his head, leaned back and closed his eyes. *Maybe Marnie had the right idea. It'd been an exhausting day; a nap couldn't hurt.*

JUST HOLD ON

CHAPTER TWENTY

Marnie lay in the silence, thinking. She knew Jake thought she was sleeping, but she wasn't. She'd shut her eyes so she could focus on what he was saying, on what he was *really* asking of her. She didn't want to admit it, but he was right. She wanted a baby; she really, *really* wanted another baby, but she'd been thinking about what *she* wanted, not what would be best for a child. She wasn't in any shape to raise a child—she could barely take care of herself.

Marnie remembered how she and Daniel had discussed this same thing, long before they decided to start a family. Back then, they both agreed to wait until after they were married to have children, because they both thought it was important for the child to have that security, to know both its parents were committed to each other. She knew, in her heart, that she still believed that would be the best way—she just craved motherhood so badly. She missed it so much—she missed Katie so much.

Marnie knew too, Jake was right about her feelings for him. She really *did* love him, and not only because he'd taken care of her over the past year. Although, in all honesty, the fact he *had* behaved as he did probably did have a lot to do with her feelings. She considered this for a few moments and thought the events of the last year showed Jake's character more thoroughly and honestly, than would have been possible in a typical relationship.

What if they'd met each other out in the street one day and began dating, like—well, like normal people would do? She would've certainly missed out on so much of the real him. To a casual observer, Jake seemed shy, quiet and somewhat socially awkward. Attractive certainly, but easy enough to dismiss. He was so much more than that, though.

This shy, quiet man who'd burst through a door to try to save a stranger, then had heroically given what little breath he had to a little girl he didn't know in an effort to save her life. He carried Marnie, quite literally, through the devastating first months after the fire, fed her with care, bathed her tenderly and brushed through massive amounts of tangled hair. He then, continued with the care, as he sung to her, read to her and sat up with her when she couldn't sleep, held her when nightmares infested her sleep and left her shaken and vomiting.

Jake consistently put her needs before his own, even when he hadn't known her. He loved her when she couldn't even speak to him. He'd given up his own life to take care of her, without any promise of reciprocation. He wasn't a perfect man...she guessed no man really was, but Jake was a *good* man. A man with integrity, with character. Honest, solid, stable.

Maybe their relationship did move a little bit faster than usual, but then again, they'd crammed a lifetime worth of tragedy and obstacles into one short year. Their relationship was certainly unconventional, but it didn't mean they couldn't build on what they'd started. It didn't mean they couldn't be happy together.

Marnie opened her eyes, to gaze up at him. Her head was against his chest and she listened to the steady rhythm of his heartbeat. His arms were still tightly wrapped around her and she let herself relax enough to feel, really *feel*, the strength in those arms. She always felt safe in his arms. Marnie guessed it's because she knew, without a doubt, no matter what happened, he would be there. Caring for her, looking out for her, loving her. Always. She felt cherished. He had said it—he just said he loved her.

Marnie smiled. *Yes*, she thought. Yes, she did love this man. Even more than that, she almost felt certain she was *in* love with this man, but she wasn't going to tell him, not just yet. Marnie wanted to take some more time, search her heart. She needed to be sure, completely sure, before she told him. She understood what he meant, about Daniel.

Marnie's eyes watered. God, she missed Daniel so much.

Just after Daniel died, she'd seen him everywhere. Walking down the street, at the grocery store, driving down the expressway. She would walk into their bedroom, and for just a moment, she could

JUST HOLD ON

see him lying there, tangled up in the blankets, his lips curved into a smile as if he were dreaming of something pleasant. She would stop and hold her breath, like she thought somehow, if she held very still and didn't breathe or make any noise, he wouldn't disappear. But he did—he always did.

And every time, every single time, it tore her heart from her chest and ripped it to shreds. It'd been one of the reasons she decided to move. At the old place, every room held memories. A hundred times a day, she relived the pain of Daniel's death over again.

Now though, now she had the opposite problem. Now, she would close her eyes and try to remember the exact shade of Daniel's eyes, the set of his jaw when he was concentrating hard on something, the expression of perfect joy on his face the morning Katie had been born, and—she couldn't do it. She could conjure a picture up in her mind, but she knew it wasn't right.

Some days, she wanted to recall the sound of his voice—it was gone. *Why?* Why couldn't she remember? *What did that say about her?* She wondered. Did it mean she didn't love Daniel anymore? Maybe she hadn't loved him enough to begin with, if she could forget him so easily.

No—Marnie knew that wasn't true. She *had* loved Daniel; she loved him with everything she had. She believed they would stay together forever, that they would grow old together, but now, some days, it was like she'd forgotten he had died.

Then something would remind her of Daniel and she would remember that day in heartbreaking detail. The car pulling up the drive, the uniformed officer walking stiffly up to her door.

Her, standing at the door, holding Katie's hand as she listened to the officer's cold, hateful words. Katie innocently looking up at her, asking if Daddy was coming soon. She imagined Katie's soft baby voice saying, "Daddy? Daddy?" While hot tears splashed down her face.

Marnie tried to force her sobs into deep, steady breaths.

Jake's arms tightened around her, squeezing her, reminding her he was still here.

JUST HOLD ON

Abruptly, she felt warm and safe again, even in his sleep, he was taking care of her.

CHAPTER TWENTY-ONE

Marnie had no idea what Jake was up to. There was something weird going on, she felt certain of it. He couldn't sit still, he constantly seemed to be walking out of the apartment to talk on his cell phone…he seemed much more scatterbrained than usual. And he kept asking her what she wanted for her birthday. Ice-cream cake, she'd tell him, then would turn right around and ask her again.

Tomorrow, December 13, would be her thirtieth birthday. Marnie stopped what she was doing and thought about it. This certainly wasn't the life she'd expected to have at thirty. She closed her eyes and bit her lip, hard to mentally force herself to focus on another line of thought. She found that physically shutting out anything else in the room helped, and biting her lip kind of centered her thoughts. Yes, she

JUST HOLD ON

was going through a lot of chapstick, but for the moment, it seemed to help. She felt relieved she had a home to live in; she was grateful she had Jake to lean on. She felt thankful to have food on the table; grateful for their crazy, little three-legged dog.

She took a deep breath—there. That was better. Then, she watched curiously as Jake answered another call on his cell, looked up at her, and bolted from the apartment. *Oh yes*, she thought, *he was definitely up to something.* If he thought he was being subtle, he needed a lot more practice.

Marnie found a smile had just formed on her lips.

~***~

Jake's hands were shaking, he felt so excited. While he paced in the parking lot, making arrangements to pick up Marnie's birthday present in the morning, he kept glancing behind himself nervously. He didn't want her to find out what he was doing. He'd thought about this long and hard, and now when he'd made his decision already, he wanted everything to go perfectly tomorrow.

"Yes," he spoke into the phone, "Yes, I'll be there by noon. Will everything be ready for pick up by then? Great. See you then. Bye."

When Jake placed the phone back in his pocket, he grinned. He felt so lighthearted, and just—joyous. Like a little kid at Christmas. He hoped Marnie was ready for this. He really wanted her to be happy and it felt like the right time. This gift was a big commitment, but he felt confident she was ready to take it on. Well, he corrected himself—*they* would take it on. Together. It was, after all, a lifetime commitment.

Up early the next day, Jake had already showered, dressed, and taken Barbossa out for a short walk. Marnie was still sleeping. Since he had some time to kill, he cleaned up the living room a little better, vacuumed and washed the dishes from last night's dinner. He checked the clock—still a couple hours left to wait. He sang softly to himself—what else could he do? Hmm—he could make Marnie breakfast. That would be nice and by

JUST HOLD ON

the time it was done, he could run past the bakery, pick up her ice-cream cake, then collect her gift right on time.

Wait! What if the ice-cream in the cake started melting while he was getting the present? It was cold outside, but maybe not cold enough to keep the ice-cream frozen. Maybe, he could stop at Wal-Mart, buy a cooler and ice for the cake and still make it on time.

Rapidly, he cracked a few eggs for an omelet into a pan, tossed in some ham and cheese. Popped some bread into the toaster. There...done. Jake balanced the plate on one arm, poured a glass of orange juice with the other. Twisting the bedroom doorknob with his knee, he pushed the door open and called her name. "Marnie! Happy birthday! Look, I made you a good breakfast."

Sleepily, Marnie opened her eyes and pushed her hair out of her face. She smiled and slid up into a sitting position, pushing her pillow behind her back as she did so. "Thank you, Jake. That's so sweet of you. This looks great."

Jake cleared his throat. "So hey, um, I need to leave, um, for a couple hours. I have some, um, errands to run, and then I'm going to get your ice-cream cake. Then, I'll be back and we'll do the birthday thing. Okay?" He nodded his head in answer to his own question, planted a kiss atop her head and left.

~***~

Jake is for sure, the sweetest guy in the world and he looked so proud of himself. Marnie almost laughed out loud as she watched him practically run out the door. It seemed so obvious, how he kept trying to hide something. Briefly, she wondered what the big surprise would be, but couldn't come up with anything. *Oh, well.* Marnie decided to try and just enjoy the day.

Barbossa wandered in through the open bedroom door and ambled up onto the bed. He looked first at her plate, then up at her face and back

JUST HOLD ON

again. He made a pitiful sound and flopped over on the bed.

"Oh, alright. Fine; here you go, you whiny dog. *One* bite of eggs, and that's it...no more. This is my birthday breakfast, not yours."

The little dog rolled over onto his back, pleading with his eyes for her to scratch his belly.

Laughing, she consented. Barbossa writhed with happiness. "You big, dumb dog. I bet you have no idea how much you mean to me. Come here." She pulled him closer and slid back down under the covers. It was her birthday; she should be allowed to sleep in a little bit.

Barbossa seemed to have the same idea. He was already snoring before she even closed her eyes.

~***~

Jake was anxiously rushing through Wal-Mart, mentally ticking items off an imaginary list in his head. He'd found a cake sized cooler and put in the cart. He had candles, drinks and some snacks for tonight. Chips and dip. He stopped as he rounded a corner and saw a rack of flower bouquets, then picked one up and examined it. He thought Marnie might like flowers; he'd never gotten her any, but it seemed like something a girl should like, so he chose a colorful bunch and set that carefully in his cart.

He was heading to the check-out when he remembered the ice. Grabbing a bag of it, he got in the shortest line and quickly paid for his items. Out the door, he loaded the car and headed for the bakery. The cake turned out perfectly. Jake carried it out and carefully placed it into the cooler, arranging it in the trunk so it wouldn't slide. He checked his watch…he was right on time.

Jake walked out the door of the jeweler's, whistling. He slipped his hand into his jeans pocket, felt around for the small box and smiled to himself. He was sure she would love it. One more stop to go, then home. He took a deep breath and let it out slowly. Tonight would be a big night. In his mind, it

JUST HOLD ON

all went perfectly. He hoped the reality lived up to his expectations.

~***~

Marnie sat on the couch, watching TV and waiting for Jake to get home. He'd been gone much longer than she'd expected he would be. Finally, she heard the key jiggling in the lock and looked up at him.

His face looked flushed as he balanced the cake in one hand and several bags the other.

"Hey!" she greeted.

"Hey, yourself," Jake answered. *Funny*, he'd forgotten she would be here while he was hauling everything in. How dumb could he be? How was he ever going to get everything in without her seeing? "Um, Marnie? I—I need for you to go somewhere."

"Go somewhere? Now? Where?"

"Uh—the bathroom? I need you to go to the bathroom."

"But I don't have to go to the bathroom."

"No—no—I mean, I need you to go into the bathroom, not *go* to the bathroom and shut the door. So, you don't see what I've got. It isn't wrapped yet."

"Oh! Oh. Okay. So—now?"

"Yeah…yeah. Now. Um—and you've got to stay in there. Don't come out until I tell you to. Okay?"

"Okay." This seemed weird, but she went.

Jake put the cake into the freezer and brought in the rest of the groceries. Then, he ran back out to the car and carried in her gift back. He was hoping against hope this all worked out right. There—he had everything in the bedroom, and it all seemed fine. *Just fine. Great.*

Carefully, he wrapped the bottom portion of the large box he'd carried in, and then separately wrapped the top part. It was the only way he could think of to do it. He checked the gift again…still good. *Okay, here we go.* He took a deep breath and called Marnie's name. "So, birthday girl, what do

JUST HOLD ON

you want to do first? Eat cake or have your present? Probably, the present?"

Marnie stepped out of the bathroom and walked down to the kitchen. "I think I want the cake first. That looks really good."

Jake looked momentarily crestfallen. "Oh, are you sure? Because, we could do presents first. I mean, you know, if you wanted to. Do presents first. But—whatever."

"No. No, I'm sure. It's been a long time since I've had ice-cream cake and it's my favorite thing. I definitely want cake first." Marnie knew what Jake wanted and she knew she was being a little bit mean, but gosh, it was so amusing. Watching him acting as if he didn't care one way or the other, when obviously he was antsy to give her his gift.

He rocked back on his heels and ran his hand through his hair.

"Well, okay. Um—just give me a minute here, Marnie. I need to go check on something in the bedroom. You stay out here, okay?"

"Okay." She felt puzzled, but stayed put.

That was quick—Jake came right back out. He took the cake from the freezer and lit the candles he'd stuck into it. Singing, he carried the cake to the dining table, sitting it down in front of Marnie just in time for him to finish the birthday song.

Marnie blew her candles out, then Jake cut the cake and served a slice to both of them. He finished his in about two bites, while Marnie picked at hers ever so slowly…relishing every tiny bite she took. She watched him from the corner of her eye, he seemed to be shifting from side to side in his chair. She could tell he was getting more and more anxious.

Oh gosh, now he actually seemed to be sitting on his hands. Marnie couldn't keep it up; he seemed too pitiful. She scooped up the last few bites of cake into one big mouthful, chewed, swallowed and grinned at Jake. "Alright. I can see you're antsy. Let's get this present thing over with."

Jake launched from his seat as if he'd been shot out of it. "Marnie. Okay, I want you to come sit…" He turned in a circle, surveying the room as if there

JUST HOLD ON

were countless possibilities "….here. On the couch. I think that will be best. Yes, definitely the couch."

Marnie allowed Jake to take her by the wrist and lead her to the couch, as if she couldn't possibly find her way on her own. She kept thinking earlier, how she couldn't care less what the big gift was…Just watching Jake acting like this was incredibly entertaining. She wanted to laugh, but thought she might hurt his feelings, so she remained silent.

"Okay. Are you ready?"

Marnie nodded obediently.

"Okay. Stay here. Um—and close your eyes. Keep them closed. No peeking. I'll be right back."

CHAPTER TWENTY-TWO

Marnie could feel laughter bubbling up from deep inside. She knew she wasn't going to be able to hold it in much longer. She hoped Jake would hurry up with whatever he was doing in the bedroom. *Thump*—what was that? *Oops!* She almost opened her eyes. *What in the world is Jake doing in there?*

She heard a couple more loud thumping sounds, a squeak, and then Jake hissed loudly, "Ouch! Stop it…that hurt!"

Oh dear, curiosity was about to do her in. She forced herself to keep her eyes shut tight. A few more odds sounds could be heard, and then she could hear something large dragging across the floor.

"Okay! Open your eyes, Marnie. Happy Birthday!"

JUST HOLD ON

Slowly, she opened her eyes and waited for her vision to focus.

Jake was kneeling on the floor next to a large wrapped box and he was grinning so wide, he looked a little manic. "Okay, listen. I want to tell you something. This—gift, this present—okay, before you open it, I want you to know that I've thought about this a lot and I think this is a really good idea. I mean for both of us. It's going to be a big commitment and I know it's—well, it's going to change a lot around here, but I really want you to—to keep an open mind. Okay? Okay. Well, get down here! Open it, before I open it for you!"

After listening to Jake's spiel Marnie felt truly curious and a little bit nervous. This gift would change their lives? How? The box seemed huge, surely it couldn't be a—but then again, he *was* kneeling right there in front of her—but he wouldn't ask her *that*—not now—would he? She gazed over at him.

Smiling proudly, he kept gesturing with his hands for her to open the gift.

Hands shaking, she lifted the lid tentatively and peered inside. *What is that?* Something moved. Moved? That couldn't be right. But it did, the thing; it *scurried* around inside the box. She pulled the entire lid off and stared into the box, mouth agape. A mouse—or even worse, a rat? Eww! She *hated* mice!

Beside her, Jake clapped his hands like an excited child. "Reach in, take her out!"

Her? Marnie blinked and stared down at her gift. Two tiny brown eyes met her own. *Mirf*—a tiny sound escaped from the tiny mouth. Tiny ears stood tall in tiny triangles. Everything about it...about *her*...was tiny. Marnie reached in and—oh, oh...she wasn't sure she wanted to touch it—carefully, gently, she scooped up the tiny little being and brought it out onto her lap.

"Mirf," it chirped or rather, it barked. Sort of. It curled up into a tiny ball and closed its eyes.

Marnie's wide eyes met Jake's; questioning him without having to say a word.

Jake excitedly scooted around the box, so he was sitting side by side with Marnie. He reached his

JUST HOLD ON

hand out to pet the little creature. "I was talking to the lady who runs the rescue I got Barbossa from and she told me that someone had dropped off an expectant Yorkshire terrier a couple months ago. Just dropped the poor little thing off in the middle of the night...left it in a box outside in the cold. They found her the next morning and took her in. So, anyway, she ended up having three puppies about nine weeks ago. Three girls. The rescue people were getting ready to put them up for adoption, so I went and looked at them last week. And this little girl—she just captured my heart, Marnie. Look how sweet she is. I guess she was the runt of the litter, because she's a lot smaller than the other two. They had to take extra care with her, feeding her puppy formula to get her to gain weight..." He gently patted its head as he paused.

Marnie listened but couldn't stop staring at the tiny pup in her lap.

"...I guess it was touch and go for a while, but she's doing pretty good now. We have to be careful to keep her real warm, since she's so little and we have to feed her every couple of hours, so her blood sugar doesn't drop. Are you happy? I thought—I thought—I thought you would really like her."

"So, I told you I wanted a baby, and instead, you got me a baby dog?"

"Well, not—not exactly like that. I know—I know it's not the same. Not at all. But...well, she needs us. The rescue lady told me that they had to find her a special home, a home where the owners would be there most of the day to keep an eye on her and make sure she keeps eating and stays warm. And I thought of you—or rather, of us. I mean, we're both here all day anyway. I thought we could do this together. take care of her, keep her safe, and watch her grow...."

Marnie sat very still and watched the different expression glide across his face as he talked.

"And with your birthday coming up—it just seemed so perfect. I thought it would give you—well, you know how you were saying you felt like—like you didn't have a purpose. I just thought this would give that to you. And you seem to like Barbossa so well—I thought..." Jake's voice drifted off. "Don't you like her?"

JUST HOLD ON

"No, it's not like that. I'm just surprised, I guess. I never imagined—just give me a minute to think about this." Marnie picked up the puppy and held her, looking at her face. She was kind of cute. She was so small, she couldn't weigh more than two pounds, Marnie guessed. "Does she have a name?"

"Yeah. Actually, the rescue named her, but we could always change it if you want to."

"Well, what's her name? What were they calling her there?"

"Hope. The mother dog was called Serenity and the rescue people named the three puppies Faith, Hope and Joy. I thought it was kind of fitting...Hope. And then, when I got the idea for your birthday, I thought about what you'd said back at Thanksgiving. About everything being negative, and how you wanted something positive to look forward to. I thought—what you needed was hope, and then there she was. *Hope.* It just seemed so perfect."

"I like it too, Jake. She's cute, and I'd like to keep her. I'd like to have *Hope*." Marnie laughed a little at the pun. "I've never had a puppy before. It's not something I've ever thought about doing, but I think you're right. I think it would be good for me…for us. Do you think Barbossa will like her?"

"One way to find out." Jake called the dog over.

Barbossa sniffed the little puppy, bopped her on the head with his paw, and then walked away and flopped back onto his bed.

"Well, I guess that settles that. He doesn't seem to mind her." They both laughed for a minute. "There's something else, Marnie. Did you see her tag?"

Marnie peered down at the small pink heart-shaped tag. Reaching out, she took it in her hand and looked closer. There was the little pink tag, and then a couple of silver rings. She looked again. Wait—that wasn't just a silver ring, that was a *ring*. *A real ring*. A *ring*, ring. Marnie's breath caught in her chest. She couldn't think what she should do. Her hands started to shake.

Jake reached out and unhooked the ring from the collar. "This isn't—this isn't an engagement ring. It's more—it's more, I guess, a promise ring. A promise to you. I don't know where this is going, this—between you and I. At first, Marnie, to be honest I pitied you. Then—then I thought about Cassie and I wanted to take care of you the way I would have wanted someone to take care of her, if she had been in your situation. And I did…I did look on you like that. Like a little sister, I guess. But over time, to be honest with you, my feelings have changed. I care so much for you, Marnie. You're my best friend, but you're more than that. I've never felt this level of closeness, this…easy familiarity, with anyone else. Is this—is this what being in love is like—?" He looked away as his anxious ranting paused a little.

Marnie felt like she couldn't breathe.

"—I don't know, I really don't. But—but I want to find out. I think we, I mean both of us, we've kind of been shafted. But maybe together, we could rebuild some of what we've lost. We won't, either of us, be who we were before…before we lost the ones we loved so much, but we might be able to build something different, something strong and real. See the stones? Turquoise, for your birthstone and the diamonds surrounding it are my birthstone. I want you to look at this ring and remember, always remember Marnie, that no matter what—no matter if we end up staying together, or if, down the road, we end up going separate ways—I promise always to look out for you. To be there for you if you need me, whatever, whenever. *Always*. It would mean a lot to me, Marnie, if you would agree to wear it."

He watched expectantly as she took the ring from his hand and looked at it.

After a few moments, she slipped it onto the third finger of her right hand. She blinked back some tears as she caught his eye and hoped he understood why she couldn't put the ring on her left hand.

The look in his eyes when they met hers told her that he did. "Okay! So—here's the thing. Our new puppy needs some stuff, dishes, leash, a bed. I found a little pet shop about a half hour away from here; I drove out there a couple days ago, just to see what it was like. It's pretty small and it didn't seem busy at all. I guess I could have gotten the puppy stuff while I was there, but I thought...I thought, you know? That maybe, you might like to go with me.

JUST HOLD ON

So, you could pick it all out. Do you think—do you think you'd like that?"

"Well," Marnie began slowly. "I was thinking about going to a store after the New Year, but you know what? I think I would—yes, I would like to go, as long as when we get there, it isn't filled with people. I would kind of like to pick out things for Hope, and this is a good reason to push me into going to a store. Could we go now? Before I talk myself out of it?"

"Yeah! Sure, sure. We can leave right now. Okay, let me um—well, we could put her in Barbossa's old crate while we're gone. Or, you know, they let you take dogs into the store over there. I saw lots of people do that. We could do that, if you want. Do you want to take her with us?"

Within minutes, they were out the door. It'd been a couple of months since Marnie had been out of the apartment... and she did feel nervous. She battled within herself. She knew she needed to force herself to start doing this more often, but it was so much easier to stay inside. She stopped for a moment in the parking lot and tried her trick of shutting her eyes and biting her lip, focusing on the warm squiggling bundle tucked inside her coat. Marnie made herself think about Hope—she was helpless and she needed Marnie to do this for her. Resolutely, Marnie opened her eyes and took the remaining steps to Jake's car.

They were off.

A half hour later, they pulled into the pet shop's nearly deserted parking lot. The shop looked to be a small family-owned business and the building was painted a horrific shade of bright green. A lone street light dimly lit the pavement as Jake and Marnie hurried toward the door. The bell on the door made a loud dinging sound as they walked in. Hope's face popped out the top of Marnie's coat, and her tiny head swiveled back and forth, taking in the surroundings.

~***~

JUST HOLD ON

Jake heard Marnie's sharp intake of breath, and felt her draw back, inching toward the door. "Marnie." He stepped in front of her, putting his hand on her shoulder. "Breathe. You can do this, I know you can. I'm right here." Dropping back to her side, he placed his hand on the small of her back, gently propelling her forward to the aisle marked *Dogs*.

Fortunately, they were the only customers in the store. Jake could see Marnie was physically forcing herself to take slow, steady breaths, but at least she was doing it—she was staying in the store. He knew it was hard on her, being out in public, and he felt so proud of her, he could just about cry. *There!* They'd arrived near the dog beds.

Marnie looked over the selections. "Jake? How much—how much were you thinking we should spend?"

"Choose whatever one you want. I don't care, don't worry about cost."

Marnie reached out to touch several beds before shyly pulling one from the shelf. It was tiny, fluffy and very, very pink, with *Princess* across the front.

Jake got a feeling this was the one she'd wanted all along, but she hesitated at first, because it cost a little bit more. "That's fine. Very nice." He tossed it into the cart. "Let's go look at leashes."

They turned the corner and went up an aisle filled with harnesses and leashes of just about every size and color. "The lady at the rescue said we should get her a harness, because since she's so small hooking a leash up to a collar could hurt her trachea." Jake pulled out a purple harness and leash set. "How about this one?"

Marnie nodded, but he could tell she didn't really like it. "Just tell me what one you want. Talk to me here, don't just leave me to guess. I have no idea what I'm doing."

"Well, I kind of like this one," Marnie offered in a small voice.

Oh, dear—it was pink with rhinestones. Jake sensed right then that everything they got today was going to be pink. "Fine. That's fine. Go ahead, put it in the cart. Let's see...what else do we need?"

"I—Jake?" Marnie whispered. "Can I get her a sweater? Do you think that would be silly?"

JUST HOLD ON

"Get who a sweater?"

"The puppy, Hope. In case, she gets cold. You said—you said we had to keep her warm."

"Oh. Well, I guess. I've never seen a dog sweater before. Do they really make them?"

"Yeah, I see some over there." Cradling the little dog in the crook of her arm, Marnie made her way to a rack of coats and sweaters. "Look, Jake, come here. Look how tiny these are!"

Jake was grinning as he walked over to see what she'd found. He could tell Marnie was starting to relax and getting excited about shopping. He hoped this might happen and he felt pleased to see his little plan seemed to be working. Catching up to Marnie, he looked at the many tiny sweaters she laid out in front of her. *Pink, pink, and more pink.* He sighed. "Which ones do you want?"

"Well, I thought maybe we should get a couple for her? So, she doesn't get cold? What do you think? And maybe we could get her a blanket?"

Jake wanted to laugh, but didn't dare. Instead, he nodded. "Sure, sure. Whatever, that's fine. We should pick up some dishes for her food and water and get a bag of puppy food. Barbossa eats adult food and I know we can't give her that. Oh, and a brush, since her hair is long. The rescue said it could get mats in it if we don't keep it brushed." The cart was heaping with items as he pushed it toward the check-out.

"Jake, what about a book?" Marnie stopped at a rack filled with animal care books. "Look, this would be good for us to read together. I want to make sure I'm taking care of her right, and this one is all about puppy care. We should get that and this one is all about the Yorkshire terrier breed, so we should get it too."

"Okay, sure, but we should probably get going. She's going to need to eat soon." Jake wondered how Marnie would react, once the cashier came up to the register. An older woman seemed to appear out of nowhere, but thankfully, she didn't seem to be a big talker.

Marnie kept her eyes averted and kind of rocked back and forth on her heels.

Jake flung the items on the belt and whipped out a credit card. It was over quickly, then they were outside, heading to his car in no time. Jake looked over his shoulder and smiled at the sight of Marnie holding Hope up to her face, whispering to her.

Once they were settled in the car, Jake spoke, "I think your bravery tonight deserves an award. How about we stop and get milkshakes to celebrate?"

Marnie smiled at that. "Sure," she responded, "That sounds great. As long as it isn't chocolate. I've never really cared that much for chocolate shakes."

Jake stopped for a second and slowly looked over at her, a startled look on his face...Then, he grinned at her while he shook his head and started the car.

VALARIE SAVAGE KINNEY

CHAPTER TWENTY-THREE

Christmas Eve. It was difficult for Marnie to believe that it'd only been a year ago when she'd been putting together a small bike for Katie, looking forward to watching her little girl's face light up when she found the gift Christmas morning. It seemed like it'd been at least a hundred lifetimes since that night. Facing Christmas was so hard. She didn't really want to celebrate it this year; the closer the day came, the more lost she felt.

Marnie could feel depression sapping her strength, making her feel as if every step she took, pulled at all the strength she could muster. The last few days had been particularly hard. She felt like the air surrounding her grew heavy, making her chest hurt with the effort of each breath she took. She didn't want to get out of bed, but Jake had gone to

JUST HOLD ON

visit his mother and the dogs needed to be let out. Forcing herself from the bed, she pushed herself to the living room and opened Hope's tiny crate.

It always seemed next to impossible not to laugh at the tiny body launching out the front of the crate with those tiny brown eyes looking up at her. She cradled the little, warm bundle of fur close to her chest, soaking up the comforting feeling of the small heart beating so close to her own.

After taking the dogs out and filling their dishes, Marnie's energy was just about spent. The thought of facing the rest of the day was exhausting, and she wasn't sure how she was going to make it. She didn't expect Jake to be back for a few more hours yet, and in all honesty, the only thing she wanted to do was crawl back into bed and go to sleep. Marnie whistled for Barbossa and picked Hope up into her arms, then settled them both in the bed with her. Grateful, when she felt sleep washing over her quickly.

~***~

VALARIE SAVAGE KINNEY

Jake spent most of the day at the home with his mother and although, he didn't actually *do* anything but sit with her while he was there, he became tired out from the effort. As he drove home, he thought about what he should do with Marnie tonight and tomorrow. He knew she hadn't been looking forward to the holiday and he wondered if they should even do anything at all.

Jake wanted to buy her a gift, but he felt like it might hurt her somehow. Watching her descend back into depression over the last week had been painful. Her steps had becomes lower; every effort to move appeared to be almost more than she could bear. The melancholy in the apartment was palpable…it hung thickly in the air, like hot, sticky fog on a humid July day. He could almost see it, feel it, taste it, but felt powerless to stop it. He wanted to fix it…he wanted to *do* something to make her feel better.

He'd thought and thought about it, and he came to the conclusion that the only way to help Marnie

JUST HOLD ON

through this was to do exactly that...help her. Hold her and support her until it was over. Christmas wasn't like Thanksgiving had been. Christmas this year for Marnie was a raw, painful wound that could not be glossed over with a Band-Aid of pie or presents.

 Jake hesitated outside the apartment, key in the lock. He felt, for some reason, as if he was about to enter a war zone. He took a deep breath, and turned the key. He was ready for this.

~*** ~

 Marnie heard Jake opening the door and stifled a sob. She was so sick of crying, sick of hurting so much. She wished she could just take a magic pill that would make her sleep until Christmas was over. Anxiety at the thought of making it through was forming a tight knot of dread in her stomach. The more she worried about it, the more insurmountable the problem of tomorrow became.

Marnie even considered sending Jake to the store for alcohol. If she could drink enough to blur out reality for a few days, until Christmas passed, she thought it might help. She hadn't ever been a big drinker, but maybe, this could be an exception. Just this once. But then, what if she couldn't stop? It seemed like every thought she had caused her more and more worry. Marnie squeezed her eyes shut tight. If only she could stop her thought. Stop her mind from racing in circles—stop thinking at all—just stop…

Marnie felt rather than heard Jake enter the room. She felt him pause in the doorway, felt his steps—one, two, three—then he paused again. Four, five, six. She felt the mattress dip under his weight, then his strong, warm arms coming around her; pulling her towards him. Felt his hot breath on her neck as he whispered, "I'm here, I'm here." Marnie felt loved, and she felt a tiny bit of the concrete block of anxiety in her gut chip away.

~***~

JUST HOLD ON

Jake stood in the bedroom doorway, watching Marnie struggle. He could hear her whispering to herself, trying to swallow the sobs so they eventually sounded like strangled hiccups.

For a fleeting second, just a second, he could identify with his father. Loving Marnie so much and watching her struggle so obviously, hurt him. It hurt him more than dealing with his own pain. Was that why his father had left? Because, watching his mother struggle had hurt him this way?

Jake shook his head. That is no excuse; it was cowardly. As much as it hurt, Jake knew Marnie needed him. He had to think about what she needed, not what would be easier for him.

Late into the night, they were both still awake, lying in bed. Marnie whispered, "Jake, I can't do this. I can't face it—tomorrow. I can't, I can't."

Jake pulled her closer to him, and waited a few minutes before answering, "I know. I know it's hard. I'll be here though, I won't leave. It doesn't have to be any different than any other day. If you want, we can just stay in here all day, not even think about it. We could read a book, or play games, or we could watch movies. Anything...Marnie, what can I do? How—what can I do? How can I help you through this?"

He gazed down at her. Her head was nestled into the groove between his shoulder and chest...her eyes were wet with unshed tears. She fit so perfectly against him and lying there, he thought he wanted to go to bed and wake up like this every day for the rest of his life. Jake tipped his head so that he could kiss her forehead. "Anything. I want to help you. Just tell me. I want to make you feel better."

"You can't," Marnie spoke up rather than whispered this time, and her voice Sounded flat, hard. "I can't feel better. This hurts. *I* hurt. There is nothing you can do, unless—unless you are willing to help me get drunk...absolutely loaded enough to numb my mind. That might help."

"Do you really think it would help? I don't think it would, baby. I think it would just make you feel worse."

JUST HOLD ON

"I thought you said you'd do anything for me. Anything! Anything but that, huh? Fine. Just leave then. Leave me alone." Marnie twisted her body to the other side of the bed, yanking the blankets with her.

Jake waited quietly.

"Jake, wait. I need you. Don't leave. Please, please don't leave? I don't want to be alone with this."

"Okay. Okay, I'm here. I'm staying. I'm right here, Marnie." Jake reached out to touch her face, and with his thumb he wiped away a tear that had spilled over. "I'm not going anywhere."

CHAPTER TWENTY-FOUR

A new year. Jake found it difficult to believe everything that happened over the last year. New Year's Eve—almost an entire year since the fire and so much had changed for both of them. It seemed staggering really, how much had happened. Tonight, would be a new start, a time to move forward. A time for more changes.

Jake hummed to himself as he started the timer and placed dinner in the oven. Nothing fancy, but he was looking forward to the evening. They were staying home and hanging out, but Marnie seemed to be doing a lot better.

Christmas had been tough and for a few days after she still floundered, struggled. The last couple of days, though, she'd been up, animated and talking. Eating. Spending a lot of time with her new puppy.

JUST HOLD ON

Jake knew she thought she was weak, but watching her sink into and fight her way out of depression was impressive. He admired her strength…she was amazing. She was beautiful. She was everything.

Everything.

Marnie set the table as she watched Jake finishing up dinner. He was so strong, steady. She thought back over the last few days and knew, without a doubt, she could never have made it through last week—really, the last year—without him. She felt good about the coming year. It would be hard, it would always be hard, but Marnie felt like she was beginning to see a future for herself. She'd been thinking about taking a class at the local college. She wanted to do something, she just wasn't sure what. She'd thought about talking to a counselor at the school and she planned to discuss it with Jake tonight.

She had a lot she wanted to talk to Jake about tonight.

What was he doing? Marnie heard a thud in the living room, and peeked in.

VALARIE SAVAGE KINNEY

The dogs were crated, the furniture was moved against the walls. Jake was bending down, changing the radio station.

"What's all this?" she asked, walking into the room.

Jake stood, smiled and took her hand. "I thought I would take you dancing tonight." He drew her near, and their bodies fell into a steady rhythm as they slowly danced around the small living room in which they'd spent so much time over the last year. *Green River Ordinance* came over the speakers, and Jake started singing along, singing to Marnie…singing to their future.

"*Put on your old black dress and grab your dancing shoes…Head out to the old bar Rose, and dance away our blues…Spent all week waiting, now my mind's on you…Hold my loving arms, my loving arms are for you, yeah…Forget about all the things that we can't make right…Put on a little Emmy Lou, and your dancing shoes tonight…Hhhmmm…In a world, that gets lost in making plans…Just be my woman, yeah and I will be your man, yeah….*"

JUST HOLD ON

EPILOGUE

Jake felt her stir in bed beside him, and turned to watch her waking up. He never grew tired of this—watching her wake slowly every morning.

Her eyes fluttered and she smiled up at him.

He reached out to touch her hair, her curly dark-brown hair spilling across the pillow in a tangled mess.

Her dark eyes met his.

"Morning, sweetheart." Jake slipped his hand under her head, sliding his fingers through the curls. Every day it seemed new, this realization that she was his. *His.* Forever. How had his life ended up here?

"Daddy!" She giggled when Jake's hand snaked beneath her and slid over to her most ticklish spots. "Where Mama?"

"School. Then, she has work for a little bit, so it's just you and me for a while. What do you want to do?"

"Doggies?"

"Okay. You want to help me walk them, after breakfast?"

"Yes! Yes!"

Jake scrambled eggs, and kept an eye on Sophia as she dumped a pile of Legos on the floor. *Three years.* Some days, it was difficult to believe she was already three years old, and other days, it seemed hard to remember she hadn't always been there. He smiled—he loved this little girl so much, sometimes it actually pained him.

He glanced at the clock, mentally calculating the day ahead. He knew Marnie wouldn't be home for at least five hours. She had class until noon, and then she usually spent an hour or two at work.

She'd put so much into the charity she started, but it was a good cause. Katie's Hope provided wish trips for children who survived serious burn injuries. It was a good way to keep Katie's memory alive, and Jake felt so proud of Marnie. "Want to go to the park this morning?"

"Doggies?" Sophia wondered, wide eyed.

Jake had to laugh. Sophia loved those dogs as much as her mother did. "Yes, doggies. They can come, too."

Jake then got an idea. He pulled his cell phone from his pocket and sent a quick text.

A few minutes later, it buzzed an answer back to him and he turned back to Sophia. "How about Mommy? Want Mommy to come, too?"

"Yes! Yes!"

Jake felt glad Marnie's schedule was somewhat flexible and she could meet them after her class to spend a little time together.

About ten minutes later, he was holding the double leash for the dogs in one hand, and pushing Sophia on the swing with the other, Jake watched the gate to the park. Is that her? He squinted against the sun and looked again.

The woman walked a little closer—yes, yes, it was. After all these years, his heart still did a little flip-flop when he saw her coming toward him. He loved the way she walked so confidently...shoulders back, chin up, ready to take on the world. God, he loved her so much. His wife. His *wife*!

Marnie took the last remaining steps toward them, and stood up on her toes just a bit to offer Jake a kiss.

"Mommy!" Sophia squealed, and hopped off the swing to hug her mother's leg.

Jake pulled his wife toward him and let his hand rest on her belly for a moment. She wasn't showing yet, but she would be soon. Jake looked down at his daughter, and back up to his wife. *Marnie.* She was amazing, beautiful. *Everything.* He loved the way the sun was shining on her long red hair. He felt so relieved she'd grown it back out—it was down past her hips now.

Beautiful.

Their life together seemed so perfect, so full—so *right*. Jake felt grateful for it, for every moment. He wrapped his arms around them both and held on.

....He just—held on.

JUST HOLD ON

Valarie Savage Kinney is a writer, fiber artist and Renaissance Festival junkie with a wicked caffeine addiction. She resides in Michigan with her husband, four children, and two insane little dogs. Her work has appeared in *The Prague Revue* and *IG Living* magazine and her blog, "Organizing Chaos (and Other Misadventures)" is available for your viewing pleasure on WordPress. Valarie can be followed on Twitter @kinneychaos.

VALARIE SAVAGE KINNEY

Made in the USA
Charleston, SC
04 March 2016